joy
three Christmas stories

Angela Amman
Mandy Dawson
Cameron D. Garriepy

Joy: Three Christmas Stories

Cover Design © 2017 Bannerwing Books

Stock cover image courtesy of Brigitte Tohm via Unsplash under a Creative
Commons Zero license.

www.BannerwingBooks.com

For our families and our readers.

To get the full value of joy you must have someone to divide it with.
— Mark Twain

Also by Angela Amman

Garden Boulevard, *coming 2018*
Nothing Goes Away
In Her Hands, Metaphysical Gravity
Flutters, Echoes in Darkness
Upon A Midnight Clear, Merry Little Christmas: Three Christmas Stories
Sweet Silver Bells, Secret Santas: Two Christmas Stories
Christmas on the Lanai, Atlantic to Pacific: Two Christmas Stories

For more collections featuring Angela's work, visit her on Amazon.com.
•
Also by Mandy Dawson

Elemental Escape, *coming 2018*
Elemental Awakening
Home, Metaphysical Gravity
Awakening, Echoes in Darkness
The Rarest Gift, Merry Little Christmas: Three Christmas Stories

For more collections featuring Mandy's work, visit her on Amazon.com.
•
Also by Cameron D. Garriepy

Back Cove: A New England Seacoast Romance, *coming 2018*
Sweet Pease: A Thornton Vermont Novel
Damselfly Inn: A Thornton Vermont Novel
From the Earth to the Moon: A Thornton Vermont Story
Buck's Landing: A New England Seacoast Romance
Valentine, Metaphysical Gravity
Requiring of Care, Echoes in Darkness
Star of Wonder, Merry Little Christmas: Three Christmas Stories
Santa's Photographer, Secret Santas: Two Christmas Stories
Merry's Christmas, Atlantic to Pacific: Two Christmas Stories
Twelve Days 'Til Christmas
Closing Shift

The Children of the Parallels
Part One: Parallel Jump
Part Two: Parallel Hunt

For more collections featuring Cameron's work, visit her on Amazon.com.

CONTENTS

Christmas 2017

Merry Christmas!
♡ Cam

joy

three Christmas stories

Cameron D Ganiepy

TRUSTING STARLIGHT
by Mandy Dawson

Sami speared the three angelic smiles beneath three sets of innocent eyes with her best Mom Look. "I mean it," she hissed, "behave or I'll…" She searched her mind for a proper punishment.

"You'll beat us?" Ben asked. His eyes widened a split second too late for it to be genuine.

"Don't tempt me," Sami muttered, reaching for the door handle.

"Torture, Mommy? Will you torture us?" Penny pulled at her purse to get Sami's attention as she turned the knob in her hand. The strap dug into Sami's shoulder and sent a twinge of pain into her neck. She let the door close again and reached up to rub the muscles, wishing massages hadn't disappeared from her life along with manicures, a three bedroom house, reliable childcare, and her husband.

"I'm not going to torture you." Sami closed her eyes and counted to four. She'd given up on having a chance to make it to ten sometime between the births of Penny and Archie. Sami opened her eyes. *Archie.*

Her hand slipped from the door knob as she spun

around. Eyes flying over the quiet parking lot, she spied a splash of bright blue cotton pants disappearing under a rosemary bush. "Stay here," she called over her shoulder as she ran across the pavement. She reached out a hand and snagged the elastic band of Archie's cotton pants. "Not so fast, mister."

She brushed dead leaves from the white blond hair flopping over a face that was twisting into what she knew would be a tantrum. "No." She kept her voice firm as she hefted his squirming body onto her hip. She adjusted him when he started to slip. "I'm serious, Archibald Taylor Daily. Now is not the time for a fit." She didn't question the happy miracle when her tone of voice actually worked.

She walked toward the door where her oldest two children waited with varying degrees of patience. Penny scuffed her sneakers against the brick wall of the building while Ben... "Ben!" Sami's voice pitched to the cross between a squeak and a shout that made her sound like her own mother. "Put," she consciously lowered her voice, "the lizard down."

"He shouldn't be here, Mom." Sami ignored the twinge she felt every time he called her that. At nearly nine, he was, he'd told her, too old to call her mommy like a baby. "It's too cold. Lizards like the heat."

"Just put him down," she said, letting Archie slide down her body to the ground, but keeping a firm grip on his chubby hand.

"He'll die!" Penny said, crocodile tears welling up in her eyes.

"He's not going to die," Sami answered with what she hoped was not the last scrap of patience she had left. It was nearly four and she'd been up since before dawn trying to write her term paper before rushing the kids to school and daycare and herself to class. All she wanted to do was go home, put her feet up on the footstool she pretended was a coffee table, and pour a glass of wine all the way to the top. Instead, she had another seven hours of work in front of her before she could fall into bed and sleep. Thank God tomorrow was Saturday and it was going to be kid free.

Guilt burned and she shifted her face into a smile to hide the traitorous thought from the three children waiting for her verdict. She loved them, with all her heart, but she was tired. So very tired.

"Ben," she said, digging deep for calm, "the lizard wouldn't be here if it was dangerous. Maybe he's just heading home and took a shortcut through the parking lot."

Ben gave her a look he'd perfected the year before. It was a look that calmly reminded her he wasn't an idiot and he wasn't a baby. Sami sighed and checked her wristwatch. It was old-fashioned in an age when cellphones were an extension of a person's hand, but she liked the cool weight of the silver watch and the way it did nothing more than tell time.

She was ten minutes late.

"Lizard. Down. Now." Ben dropped it as if it had suddenly caught fire. All three of her children knew what it meant when she stopped speaking in complete sentences. The reptile scurried away as if aware of how close it had come to being stuffed into a jar. Hitching her purse higher on her shoulder and narrowing her eyes on her progeny, Sami opened the back door to Buchons'.

The kitchen was nearly empty, most of the staff already in the dining room enjoying the family meal. Sami stored her purse in the cubby near the door and led the way to the swinging door separating the kitchen from the front of the house, noting the lingering smell of cumin and chilies. She smiled. Carlos had made *pozole*.

She'd worked at the restaurant for eighteen months, finding the waitressing job shortly after The Announcement. Two years ago, she'd never thought she'd be waiting tables to put herself through grad school. Of course, two years ago, she had been a PTA mom who lived in a typical suburban neighborhood with a slightly better than typical tract home, busy planning a clever family holiday photo.

"Sami!"

She grinned at the man setting plates of sliced avocado and radishes on the center of a table crowded with her co-workers. "Hey Carlos. Sorry I'm late." The buzz of conversation barely registered a lull as approached the table.

Carlos spied the blonde trio trailing her like ducks and raised a brow. "It's family meal," he said. "You're right on time. You guys hungry?"

"Carlos!" In seconds, her children swarmed over their friend, their words tumbling over each other. Sami tuned out as the conversations turned to lizards and started to fill bowls with the fragrant soup.

"I made tortillas." Jessa handed her a plate piled high.

"Thanks," Sami said with a smile for her friend. Jessa rubbed her shoulder and sat down, not asking the question she could read on the rest of the staff's faces. *Again?*

"Okay, guys. You're going to love this," Carlos lifted Penny up and over the chair, seating her in front of a bowl of pozole and plate of tortillas. "Don't make that face, Centava. You always love my cooking." Sami waited for her finicky eater to protest, relaxing when Penny picked up her spoon and started eating.

"He could die," Ben told Carlos as he sat down next to his sister. He was obviously still thinking about the lizard as he absently shoved food in his mouth regaling Taylor - a new busboy - with tales of reptilian woe.

Sami tied a large cloth napkin around Archie's neck and handed him a tortilla. Franklin hated it when the kids weren't clean when he picked them up. Carlos leaned past her to drop an ice cube from a spoon into Archie's soup. Sami smiled her thanks and settled into

4

her own dinner, listening to the gossip and news with one eye watching the parking spaces out the front windows.

"He's starting to make this a habit, isn't he?" Carlos said, passing her the relish tray.

Sami scooped vegetables on top her bowl of soup and shrugged. "He's been busy." She pretended not to see the frown on his face.

"Busy or *busy*?" Jessa said from across the table. Sami narrowed her eyes and tilted her head in her kids' direction. They might not look like they were paying attention, but she'd learned the hard way that little ears were connected to big mouths.

Jessa shrugged and shook her head in apology, blonde ringlets dancing around a face that had grown a bit thinner over the last few months. Sami made a mental note to pin the woman down for a girls' night in sooner rather than later. Her brain reminded her that it wouldn't likely happen until the term was over.

"You look tired."

Sami turned her attention to Carlos. "Thanks," she said wryly. "You know how to make a gal feel good."

Carlos rolled his eyes. "You know I think you're most beautiful woman in the world. Not even blind man could resist you."

Sami laughed at his teasing, letting the warmth of flattery be balanced by her comfort in his friendship. She pretended not to see eyes that were suddenly too serious by far. Carlos was a dear friend, a younger brother. Every now and then, though, she felt something decidedly unsisterly towards him.

"Mommy?"

"Do you want more, Archie?"

"No," he shook his head. "Daddy's here."

All laughter left Sami as she followed Archie's pointed finger. Franklin was unfolding his long body from the sports car he'd purchased shortly after The

5

Announcement. Leave it to Franklin to drive with the top down in December.

Conversation around the table got louder as her friends and co-workers suddenly found something utterly fascinating to discuss. Sami knew why a moment later when another figure rose from the passenger side of the car. She felt her breaths go shallow.

She pasted a smile on her face and stood. "Your dad's here, kids. Time to go."

❄

Carlos jumped to his feet to help Sami wrangle the kids. He stopped when she put her hand on his arm. "Eat your dinner," she said. "I'm fine."

If she'd been holding up a blinking neon sign above her head, it would not have been any more obvious to Carlos that she was most definitely not fine. He'd watched the tension enter her body as the laughter left her eyes the second her ex husband had pulled up in front of the restaurant. "Let me get them boxes for their dinner," he offered.

"No. Really," she wiped soup and avocado from Archie's face, "it's fine. I'm sure Franklin is going to feed them something."

Ben groaned. "Sushi. He's going to make us eat sushi." He slumped in his chair and crossed his arms. "I hate sushi," he muttered mutinously. Carlos sent a glance to Jessa. As if reading his mind, his friend jumped to her feet and started stacking tortillas. A quick glance around the table set everyone else into motion. Like the well-oiled machine they were, his crew started packing enough food to feed a dozen children.

"Don't worry, man," Carlos told the boy, "stuff some of these tortillas in your shirt and you can eat them."

"Carlos!" Sami laughed. "Ben, do not put tortillas in your shirt," she said as the boy reached for his plate.

Carlos grinned, glad that he'd made her smile, and walked to the kitchen to grab a bag for the containers. Footsteps followed him.

"Dinner was good, Carlos."

He turned. "Thanks, Centava. I'm glad you liked it." He shouldn't have favorites, but if he did, this little girl with her white blonde braids and serious gray eyes would be his.

"Can we come again?"

"Anytime, *mija*. Anytime." He pulled on one silky braid. "You'd better get going. Your dad is waiting." He handed her the bag then leaned against the counter and watched her walk out the door.

Jessa strode through the opening before it had a chance to swing back. "I could kill that man," she seethed. Carlos crossed his arms and raised a brow. "Don't you act all cool and calm, Carlos. I know why you came back here."

"To get a bag."

"To keep from punching that idiot in the nose," she snorted.

Carlos shrugged, not denying it. He'd like nothing more than to pound an apology out of that miserable excuse of a man Sami had divorced. Jessa was quiet for a long moment. The sound of chatter hummed through the doors. Carlos glanced at the clock, calculating the time it would take to open and decided to give them another fifteen minutes. He'd been head chef of Buchons' for almost a year, taking over when Mark and Brie Buchon had sold it and downsized. "Have you heard from Brie?" Carlos asked.

Jessa glanced at him sideways before taking the change of subject. "We went to breakfast this morning, actually."

"Yeah? How's she doing?"

"Fantastic." Jessa smiled.

Carlos nodded. He liked the Buchons. He'd started

working for Mark the summer before senior year. His parents had been feuding over which alma mater he'd be attending after graduation when he'd seen a help wanted sign in the window of a little place that looked more like a sandwich shop than the top notch cafe it'd turned out to be. He'd gotten the job of dishwasher. That it made his parents grit their teeth and remind him of summer enrichment programs only made it better. By fall, he'd been helping Mark with prep and had found his calling. The Buchons were family.

Mindy popped her head into the kitchen. The redheaded hostess smirked. "The coast is clear," she said before disappearing to the front of the house again.

"You're going to have to tell her at some point," Jessa said pragmatically.

"She's not ready, yet." He thought for a moment. "How long has Mindy been here?"

"Two months, maybe three. Why?"

"Does everyone know?"

Jessa patted his arm. "Sweetie. You're not exactly subtle." She kissed his cheek and left him to his thoughts while she checked on her dough babies ready to go into the oven.

"Everyone?" he called after her.

"All but one," she said, taking the plastic wrap off her trays. "You might want to try making a move at some point."

"I'm working on it," he mumbled.

"You're not getting any younger." Jessa stacked the trays of rolls in the oven.

"Yeah, but I'm getting older." He pushed away from the counter and walked to the doorway. He lifted his hands to rest against the top of the door frame. "Time to get this show on the road," he called out. He stayed for a moment while his staff made half-hearted groans and got to their feet. He glanced out the window. Sami was still outside, her arms crossed tightly while Franklin with wildly gesticulating arms. Carlos pushed away from the door and retreated to the kitchen. Yeah. He'd like to crack the guy's skull.

After he thanked him for letting Sami go.

❄

Sami didn't even try to keep a smile pasted to her face as she walked out the front door of Buchons' to meet her ex husband. She'd given up on fake pleasantries right around the time she'd given up fake creamer. It should have gotten easier, meeting him week after week when he picked up the kids. For a while, it had. She'd thought they might even had become friends.

Except he'd fallen in love.

And she wasn't sure she ever could again.

"I want to tell everyone," he'd gushed, his eyes brighter than they'd ever been when they'd been married. "I've found The One."

She'd tried to bite her tongue, tried to maintain eye contact, but the words had slipped out. "It's pretty great when you think you've found someone to spend the rest of your life with, isn't it?"

He'd shuttered up at her bitter words, the arrogant mask he'd worn the last three years of their marriage hardening. "It is," he'd agreed. "It's wonderful to find someone who understands you." In the six months since, he'd been distant. His coldness manifesting into a fastidiousness that had leaked into his relationship with the kids. She'd spoken to him, at length, but his only reaction had been dismissal and an increase in tardiness.

She watched him now, using a napkin purloined from his glove compartment to wipe down his fidgeting son. His hair was perfect, rumpled just enough to be edgier than a man over forty should be. His shirt - a crisp pale blue - was tucked into jeans with a label she knew cost far more than the clothes he'd bought when married.

Everything about him screamed midlife crisis, especially the blond leaning against the side of the car watching the children with an amused smile.

Sami shifted her eyes, not ready to face the love of Franklin's life. "Their backpacks are in my car behind the restaurant. It's not locked." She eyed the convertible. The car seat in the back looked out of place and she wasn't certain the three kids would be comfortable shoved in like sardines. "You might want to put the top up."

Franklin rolled his eyes. "I'm not an idiot."

Sami bit back the obvious retort. "What time do you want me to come get them on Sunday?"

"About that," Franklin glanced back toward the car before leaning in to speak in a low voice, "I'm not going to be able to keep them until Sunday."

"What?"

"Well, I made reservations at this fantastic little bed and breakfast for tomorrow night."

"What?" Sami knew her voice was beginning to squeak by the way Penny glanced over at her. She and Ben were regaling their father's lover with stories about the lizard which had, Sami noted distantly, grown in size if their hand gestures were any indication.

"Well, it's our six month anniversary."

Sami leaned closer. "You knew that before today," she hissed.

Franklin shrugged, unrepentant. "I'm sure you can find a sitter."

Sami's mind raced, going through her back up childcare list, discarding one after another. One friend was out of town, another had the flu. A sudden thought struck her. "You should be finding a sitter," she said.

Franklin looked shocked. "I don't have anyone you'd allow to watch them."

Sami had to admit he was right. When he'd left her, he'd left everyone behind while he started a new life. She had a feeling if it wasn't for the kids, she'd never have seen him again.

"Hey, Frank? We should probably get going. Sami has to work and the kids are bouncing."

Franklin looked over to where Archie was rubbing his face against the previously flawless exterior of his car. "Archie!" Sami winced at the sharpness of his voice. "What the hell do you think you're doing?"

Before Sami could intercede, help came from an unexpected place. "Jesus Christ, Frank. Chill out. They're kids. Kids are messy."

"Don't roll your eyes at me," Frank said, but he calmed instantly.

"I've been telling him he needs to get on medication, Sami. His OCD is out of control right now. I'm sorry we're late. I had an appointment run over. Mrs. Hoyt had surgery on Monday and the poor thing needed a shampoo and style badly."

Sami felt herself thaw. Reluctantly. "It's okay, Mike."

"And what's this about tomorrow night, Frank? We have the kids. It's on the calendar. I know it is because I put it there."

"It's our six month anniversary," Franklin said. Sami noted he didn't get angry when Mike called him Frank.

"We'll celebrate next week," Mike said firmly.

"I'll see what I can do," Sami nearly kicked herself. She couldn't help it. She *liked* the man her ex-husband had fallen in love with no matter how hard she tried to hate him.

❅

"I really appreciate this, Brie," Sami said as Penny and Ben squeezed past the two women, nearly knocking them over. "You don't mind that it's a sleepover?" She pitched her voice over the sound of the children yelling for Santiago.

11

"Are you kidding? That's the best part. Mark's making donuts."

"For breakfast?"

"Dinner." Sami turned as Mark walked into the room, a towel thrown over his shoulder and flour dusting the tee shirt advertising his weekly cooking show. He slung an arm over Brie's shoulders. "You're going to love them, Archie, my man." Archie burrowed his head into Sami's neck.

"I'm sorry. He's been like this all afternoon." Sami kissed his forehead.

"Come here," Brie said, reaching for Archie. He shook his head and gripped Sami tighter. Over the top of his hair, she could see the clock ticking ever closer to the start of her shift.

"Archie, sweetheart, go with Miss Brie," Sami whispered into his ear. She pried him from her neck and handed him to Brie's waiting arms.

"They'll be fine," Brie assured her, her face glowing as she snuggled the little boy closer. Archie leaned his head against Brie and closed his eyes.

"I'll have my cell on me," Sami fretted.

Mark put his hand to Archie's forehead. "He's probably just tired. He was with his dad last night?"

"Yeah," Sami picked up her purse from where she'd dropped it.

"We'll call you if anything happens," Brie assured her. "Don't worry."

"Okay." Sami lingered at the door. "Penny! Ben!" Running feet and clicking nails on wood floors was her only warning before she was over run by her oldest children and a dog who could nearly look her in the eye. Santiago's wiry coat had taken on a gleam of health since he had adopted Mark almost a year ago. He slid to a halt, seeming to keep Penny from falling as she tried to jump in front of Ben. They wrapped their arms around her.

"Mark made donuts for dinner!" Penny told her, eyes

beaming.

"They're mac and cheese donuts!" Ben crowed.

"Be good, okay?" Sami kissed them and pushed the hair out of Ben's eyes. "Keep an eye on your little brother." She stepped back. Mark and Brie looked happy and comfortable, with the kids and dog circling them. She leaned in for one last kiss to Archie's cheek. He was asleep, his breaths even.

"Come at nine and I'll make you breakfast," Brie said.

"She's learning to cook," Mark said proudly.

"There's this hot chef on TV who makes it look easy," Brie teased.

"I'll see you then." Sami half ran down the sidewalk to her car, knowing she'd have to hit every green light to make it to work on time.

Sometimes, it felt like all she ever did was run late.

Franklin had been happy she'd been able to find a sitter. Mike had been annoyed. "Sami," he'd told her, taking her aside as Franklin gathered the kids' shoes and jackets, "you've got to stop letting him do this to you. I love that man. Warts and all. Which is why I'm telling you, you need to set some boundaries or he'll keep running all over you." Mike had sent a fond look to her ex husband. "He has a strong personality and you are too kind."

Sami thought of his words now. It wasn't that she was kind. God knows she'd had some very unkind thoughts about the man who'd broken her heart and destroyed her trust in men, but she had grown accustomed to being the adult in their marriage and, then, in their divorce. Maybe, she realized, it was time for her to take another step back. Franklin was Mike's problem now.

She was almost giddy at the thought. "Not my monkey. Not my circus," she whispered into the car as she pulled into the parking lot. She checked her watch. She was on time with four minutes to spare.

She flicked down the visor and applied a thin coat of

lipstick. A tap at her window had her dropping the tube in her lap. She turned to see a large shape looming beside her door. It opened.

Sami put her hand to her heart. "My God, Carlos. You nearly gave me a heart attack. What are you doing?"

Carlos stepped back as she got out of the car and then closed the door behind her. "I had to get something out of my Jeep and saw you pull in. I thought I'd walk in with you."

"Thanks." As they approached the door, he slowed to a stop. She looked at him. "What's wrong?"

Carlos cleared his throat. "I was wondering what you were doing Monday night."

"Oh!" Sami smiled. "Nothing too much. Why? Did you and Jessa want to come over and binge watch something? I was just thinking it's been too long since we've gotten together. This semester kicked my rear." Sami opened the door, wondering if she should suggest pizza. It'd be nice for Carlos not to cook on the one night a week the restaurant was closed. They could order out, maybe grab a six pack and settle in for a sci fi marathon.

Her thoughts were interrupted by Carlos's hand pushing the half open door closed again. He loomed over her, one hand holding the door closed, his muscular body as impenetrable as a brick wall. Sami started to take a half step back and then reminded herself this was Carlos.

"I was wondering if you would like to go out on Monday night."

"I guess so. Did you check with Jessa?" Sami preferred a pizza and beer at home, but Franklin had the kids and it might be nice to get out of the house.

"No," Carlos said, a look of frustration crossing his face.

Sami reached up and patted his arm. "Don't worry. I'll touch base with her tonight and see what we can figure out." Carlos was always game for whatever she and Jessa came up with. She didn't know what she would have done without her Buchons' family. The divorce - and the reason why - had rocked her circle of friends. Most had fallen all over themselves to embrace Franklin's exit from the closet, even as he distanced himself from his old life. She'd felt a bit like collateral damage, eventually drifting away from the people who told her how proud she must be.

"We're going to be late," Sami said, laughing into Carlos's frowning face. "Don't worry. No chick flicks." She ducked under his arm and reached for the door again. He stepped back, opening it and gesturing her into the bustle of the kitchen on a Saturday night.

❋

"Did you ask her?"

Carlos stared blankly at the screen in front of him. The kitchen was quiet, most of the staff long gone. He hit send on the vendor email and turned his attention to Jessa.

"Yeah."

"You don't look too happy," she noted, studying him. She wiped her forehead with the back of her hand, leaving a dusting of powdered sugar in its wake. Jessa handed him a plate of brioche con crema.

Carlos wasn't sure where he'd gone wrong. "I asked her if she had plans for Monday." He picked up the cream puff and took a bite. He moaned. "These are fantastic. Why are there leftovers?"

"I know how much you like them," she shrugged. "You seemed quiet all night and you know me. I'm a firm believer in the healing power of sugar." She reached over and snagged one of the tiny pastries. "I would have thought you'd be a little happier."

"She thinks we're getting together to watch a movie or maybe go out for dinner."

"That's not exactly bringing your romantic A game,

Carlos." Jessa scolded lightly. She took a bite and smiled. "I did good."

Carlos nodded in agreement before adding, "No. She thinks *we*," he gestured between the two of them, "are getting together with her and doing something."

"Oh," Jessa sounded almost as disappointed as he felt. Sami had worked at Buchons' for nineteen months, three weeks, and four days. He'd been in love with her for nineteen months, three weeks and two days. His father had always told him Hernandez men fell hard and fast and when they did, there was never another woman for them. His father had been right.

Jessa took off her apron and folded it over her arm. "She's still here, you know."

Carlos looked at her in surprise. He'd left the kitchen before closing, wanting to take care of the paperwork that was the only part of the job he didn't like.

"I made her a pot of hot chocolate and a plate of these. You weren't the only one quiet tonight." Jessa leaned down and kissed his cheek. "Go try again."

As she stood, Carlos caught her hand. Her eyes were sad, their normal spark absent. "You okay?"

She shrugged. "I will be." She smiled, a faded version of her typical brightness. "It's not a big deal, just tired."

Carlos squeezed her hand and nodded. "Go. Get some sleep." He frowned as she left the office. Jessa was the older sister he'd always wanted, even if she was closer to his mother's age than his. He worried over the lines that had appeared around her eyes over the last few months, the distance she'd put between them. Sighing he stood. She'd tell him what was going on when she was good and ready and not a minute before. He walked out of the office, flicking the light and sending the room into darkness.

The kitchen was empty. The bank of lights were turned off; the only illumination came from the old wooden table in the corner. Sami was seated beside it, her apron hanging on the back of the chair she'd pulled up to prop her feet on. A cup of steaming chocolate and a plate of mostly eaten pastries were at her side. She held a dogeared novel in her hands. She glanced up and smiled as he neared.

"Hey," she said, lifting her feet off the chair and pushing it toward him.

Carlos sat and reached for the book she held lightly and reading the cover. "Is it any good?"

She shrugged, a pale pink blush coloring her cheeks. "It's a lust in the dust book, but I love it."

He laughed. "Lust in the dust?"

"My college roommate found my stash of historical romances and, after seeing Fabio on the cover in nothing but chaps with a rearing horse in the background, dubbed it lust in the dust. I haven't been able to think of them as anything else since." She pushed the plate across the table. "Did Jessa bring you some?"

"Yeah," Carlos said, helping himself to one anyway.

"If you want to get out of here, I can box these up." Sami started to stand.

"I'm in no hurry," he said. He didn't add that he could sit and watch her eat cream puffs and read romance novels all day.

Sami folded a corner down and set the book on the table. "If I go home, I'll just start laundry and dishes and I'll never read."

Carlos studied her in silence while she sipped her cocoa. She wasn't his normal type. He'd always gone for sleek brunettes, athletic women who'd gone on runs with him in the mornings and fallen into bed with him at night, always leaving before dawn. At twenty-six he'd been more interested in having fun than having a relationship. Then this curvy woman had walked into the restaurant, white blonde hair cut just below her ears, sadness in her eyes, and three kids who were a walking advertisement for commitment.

He'd been a goner.

Sami sighed and stretched, the arching motion straining the buttons on her shirt. Carlos liked to think he was a modern man, a feminist, if his mother had anything to say about it, but he couldn't keep his eyes from straying, half hoping a button would pop. "I should really get going," she said, bringing his eyes back to her face.

"Let me lock up and I'll walk you out." He left her to go to the office, grabbing his jacket off the hook and listening to the sound of her washing the plate and mug. It would never occur to her to leave them for the next day.

He joined her at the door and set the alarm. They walked in silence to her van. She paused at door. "Thanks, but I think I'm good from here. Goodnight." She smiled and started to turn.

"Sami?"

"Hm?" She looked over her shoulder.

"Would you like to go out on a date with me Monday night?"

Her mouth dropped open and her purse fell to the ground. As answers go, it wasn't very flattering. Carlos waited, his stomach in knots.

"A date?" she squeaked.

"A date." He didn't want there to be any confusion this time.

"With me?" She touched her hand to her chest.

"With you," he said firmly.

Her mouth opened and closed before opening again. "Carlos, I'm old enough to be your mother."

"You're ten years older than me," he said dryly.

"I can't be your type," she said.

"How do you know what my type is?" He leaned against the back door of her van.

She looked at him pointedly. "I highly doubt your type drives an Odyssey."

Carlos shrugged, trying not to let on how close he was to getting on his knees and begging her to give him a chance. "I like minivans."

"You can't be serious," her voice took on the high note of panic he knew all too well. He straightened.

"Hey." She jumped when he touched her shoulder. "It's just a date," he told her, dropping his hand. "It's okay if you say no." *Please don't say no.* He held his breath.

"Just a date?"

"Yes."

"What if it doesn't work out?"

His heart started to pound. That wasn't a no. "We've been friends a long time, Sami. That's not going to change."

"You're my boss."

"Not really," Carlos shrugged. "Technically, I only manage the kitchen staff." He waited, giving her time to think.

"Okay," she finally said.

"Really?"

"Yes," she said emphatically. "I'll go on a date with you."

❉

Sami stood in front of the mirror in her bra and panties trying to figure out a way to cancel on Carlos without hurting his feelings. There was no way in hell she could go on a date with him.

Being his friend was easy. He was kind, sweet, and had a great sense of humor. She sat on the edge of her bed and rubbed her stomach. She had to cancel. And soon. He was due to pick her up in less than two hours. She flopped back on her bed.

What had she been thinking to say yes? She put her arm over her eyes and pressed until she saw white spots.

She wasn't ready to date. Just the other day she'd accidentally checked the married box on an online survey. Sami stretched and reached for the phone she'd tossed onto the bed after she'd gotten out of the shower. She was going to cancel. She'd tell him she was sick.

She coughed, experimentally, into the silence of the room. Did that sound fake? Maybe she'd say that she hadn't been able to find childcare. The risk there, of course, was that he'd offer to come over and what would she say when he showed up and she didn't have the kids?

She dropped her hand, still clutching the phone, and stared at the ceiling.

Carlos wasn't just nice, he was hot. The kind of hot even her younger self would have admired from a distance before focusing her attention on a more attainable man. *Like Franklin*. She groaned. She was not ready to date. She picked up her phone again. Texting seemed rude. She chewed her lip and studied the screensaver with its three smiling faces staring back at her. She didn't think she'd be able to handle the disappointment in his voice when she canceled.

She'd handle it worse if there wasn't any disappointment, she admitted to herself.

She jumped as the phone in her hand rang. Sighing, she answered.

"You're not going to cancel on him."

"Hi, Jessa."

"I'm serious, Sami. You are not going to cancel on him."

"I wasn't," she hedged.

"Bull."

"I'm not ready to date," Sami whispered.

"You are."

Sami stared at the ceiling, willing the moisture in her eyes away. "Jessa," her voice broke, "what if it's awful?"

"Oh sweetie," Jessa's voice poured over her like warm honey. "It's Carlos. You'll have fun."

"What if it *isn't* awful?" Sami's voice broke. She willed herself not to cry and run her mascara.

"A not awful date isn't a bad thing," Jessa said gently. "You're allowed to date. You're allowed to be happy."

"I know," Sami said. She was quiet for a moment before adding, "I don't know what to wear." She sat up on the bed and stared into her closet, knowing she'd sealed her fate. Any cold feet she might have had were being held to the fire.

"Wear something comfortable. Put on some make-up. Curl your hair. It's Carlos. He's seen you at your worst," Jessa reminded her.

Two months ago, Carlos had dropped off Tylenol for the kids after his shift, staying when he'd realized she was running a fever as well. "It's Carlos, Jess. *Carlos*."

Jessa laughed. "What are you worried about, then?"

"I hadn't ever thought of him as anything but a friend."

"Really?" Jessa drawled.

Sami felt the heat rise in her face. "Well, usually," she mumbled.

Jessa laughed. "Get dressed, Sami. And for God's sake, don't cancel on the poor guy."

"I won't," Sami promised, hanging up the phone. Taking a deep breath, she stood and went to her closet. Being married to a gay man may not have been good for her self esteem, but her wardrobe had certainly benefited. She dug through her clothes until she found what she was looking for. Pulling it out, she held it in front of her and looked in the mirror. A white tag still dangled from the sleeve.

Franklin had bought it for her the last Christmas they'd been together. She'd taken one look at the silky fabric and burst into tears, knowing the size on the tag would never fit over hips and belly still rounded from her last pregnancy. Franklin had handed her a membership card for the gym and told her she needed to stop letting herself go. She'd never hated him more, but she couldn't bring herself to throw away the gorgeous dress.

Now, though, with two years of too many missed meals and a pair of Spanx, it might just fit. She took it off the hanger and pulled it over her head. It didn't float over her body, but slid over her curves before settling in place. She looked in the mirror, turning to the side and sucking in her breath.

The deep blue material turned her eyes cobalt and made her platinum hair shine. The bodice crossed between her breasts and ended at a thick black band before flaring gently to her knees. Dropping to her knees in front of her closet, she dug into the back until she found a dusty shoe box. She pulled out the black velvet heels she'd bought before running after children determined her footwear. She stood, putting them on and taking a black cardigan off its hanger. She looked in the mirror and, for the first time, began to feel a twinge of excitement rather than panic. She didn't look half bad.

She wasn't going to curl her hair, but, she decided, the occasion called for perfume. Just a spritz on her wrist before putting on her grandmother's silver heart pendant and her mother's diamond stud earrings. She smoothed on her lipstick and stood in front of the mirror again.

She looked, she realized, almost pretty. She smiled. It was only Carlos. How bad could it be?

❄

This was, Carlos thought, the worst date he'd ever been on. He picked up his fork and speared a cucumber from his salad. If the look on Sami's face was any indication, she agreed.

He wasn't sure where it had started to go wrong. He'd knocked on her door right on time. She'd answered and, in the brightly colored light of the Christmas tree in her living room, had taken his breath away. Her eyes had been brighter. She'd done something magical to her lips that made them look pouty and utterly kissable. He'd glanced up, hoping to find mistletoe, disappointed when it wasn't conveniently there. She'd smiled. He'd smiled. He'd thought it was going to be a magical night.

He was wrong.

He'd held the car door for her and then closed it when she slid into the seat. Walking around the hood, he hadn't been able to make his grin disappear. He'd gotten in the car, the scent of citrus and flowers filling the air. It had been intoxicating.

"You look amazing," he'd said, starting the engine.

The compliment didn't land easily. "Thanks," she'd said, plucking at her dress. Their conversation on the way to the restaurant had been stilted, nothing like the usual easy flow between the two of them. His attempts at flirtation had fallen flat. Her answers to his questions had been monosyllabic.

Now, they sat like strangers rather than friends, each of them picking at the food on their plates. He glanced up and caught her eyes flitting around the room, as if looking for an escape. He grimaced. "This isn't going very well, is it." He kept it a statement of fact rather than a question.

Her face turned pink. "I'm sorry. I'm out of practice."

"Me too." His answer surprised a direct look from her. He shrugged. "It's been a while." He pushed his salad plate away as the main course arrived at their table. He eyed the plate with a professional eye and then, finding it as good a dish as he would put out, picked up his silverware.

"I'm not sure I'm ready to date," she told her plate of lobster ravioli. Carlos's hands froze, the knife and fork poised over his steak. She pushed a plump pocket to the side, leaving a trail in the cream sauce. "It's only been two years."

Carlos set his utensils down. "Hey." Sami glanced up. "It's me, here. I know." The corner of her lips quirked in a sad smile. "I *know*, Sami. You don't have to explain anything to me." He reached across the table and covered her hand with his. "How about we call this date officially over and just have dinner. You and me. Just friends."

A genuine smile split her face and her shoulders relaxed. "That's a great idea. I'm sorry, Carlos."

He shrugged again and picked up his silverware, slicing into the medium rare steak. His timing was off. He could be patient. He checked himself when he realized he was sawing at the meat a little roughly. He may not like it, but this woman was worth the wait.

✳

"Mom! Look! It's Carlos."

Sami turned in the direction Ben pointed. Carlos's unmistakable silhouette stood almost a full head above the crowd gathered in the town square waiting for the snowfall heralding the opening of Winter Wonderland.

The Christmas Eve festival promised hot cider, lights, caroling, and the new family traditions Sami was determined to create. "I think it is," Sami said, tightening her grip on Archie's hand in the crowd. Penny leaned against her side. Her suggestion that they go say hi froze on her lips as Carlos's head bent down to say something to the petite brunette next to him.

The woman turned and laughed, her profile perfection and her face filled with love. Unexpected jealousy churned Sami's stomach.

It had been two week since their disastrous date had ended with a smile and a hug. Two weeks of working together as if nothing had occurred between them. If she'd been worried about losing his friendship, the last two weeks had proven he regretted whatever impulse had caused him to ask her out in the first place. It was obvious he thought of her as nothing but a friend.

Which is why she'd noticed nothing except his broad shoulders, his easy grin, and the warmth in his eyes.

Sami sighed. She was being ridiculous and she knew it. "Let's go say hi," she told her children. They wove through the crowd until they were within arm's reach.

"Sami!" Carlos leaned to give her a kiss on the cheek. "I didn't know you would be here."

Sami eyed the beauty at his side. She was exactly what she'd envisioned Carlos's girlfriend to be: trim, gorgeous, young.

"This is Arabella," Carlos said, pulling the woman forward with an arm wrapped around her shoulders.

Sami pasted a smile on her face and wished she wasn't wearing an oversized flannel and jacket and instead looked half as stylish as the woman reaching for her hand with real warmth.

"It's nice to meet you." Sami had perfected the art of the false greeting while married to Franklin.

"I've heard so much about you," Arabella gushed.

Sami's cheeks warmed. What had she heard in the secret conversations between lovers? She wanted to say she'd never heard of the woman, but pettiness was ten years and three children ago. Instead she smiled.

"Bella wanted to check out the snow," Carlos said.

Instantly, Sami's shoulders relaxed. Bella. "I've heard so much about you too," she said honestly, smiling fully at Carlos's favorite cousin.

Penny, not to be ignored, pushed her way between the adults. "Mama said it was going to snow, Carlos!"

Carlos laughed and lifted her high above his head, setting her on his shoulders. Sami bit back a protest that she was too big, realizing that to him, she'd always be small. Bella wrapped her arms around Sami in a tight hug, whispering in her ear. "I'm so glad to meet you, finally." Bella pulled back and leaned down. "This must be Archie. Have you seen the snowmen?" Archie shook his head, his natural shyness evaporating in the warmth of her voice. "Come! I'll show you."

Archie looked to her with hope in his eyes. Sami nodded and the two of them disappeared into the crowd. She was left with Ben at her side and Penny on Carlos's shoulders, her arms wrapped loosely around his neck. They looked, she realized, like a family. She pushed the thought back into the recesses of her mind and instead focused on the present.

"Are you going to the Misfit Christmas?" Carlos asked referencing the Christmas dinner Mark Buchon had started a year before.

"We are," Sami confirmed, ticking another tradition off her growing list. "What about you?"

"My family has a huge fiesta," he said with a laugh. "We're misfits too, but all related in some way."

"That must be nice," Sami said, wistfully, shifting in the crowd, "having a big family at the holidays."

"Nice and chaotic," Carlos grinned. "There will be at least forty of us, cousins siblings, grandchildren, friends, and people who I think just wander in."

They were quiet a moment until Carlos reached out, tentatively, "You could come."

"To your family's house for Christmas?" Panic surged.

"There will be so many people there and we're friends, right?"

"Well, yeah," Sami said, hesitating. For some reason, since their date, she hadn't felt like friends. It had felt like something…more.

"Then come. My mom is making tamales." As if guessing the moment she started to fold, he added, "She only cooks once a year. Miss it now and you won't get tamales until next Christmas."

"Can we go, Mama!" It was Ben's pleading that made her cave. His slip into 'mama' melted her like hot butter.

"What can I bring?"

Carlos knew her better than anyone else. "Bring cookies. And wine. There can never be too much of either."

Sami smiled slowly. "We'll be there."

❅

"I like her, *mijo*." Julia Hernandez stirred the ponche simmering on the stove as laughter came from the other room.

"Me too, Mom." Carlos took the ladle out of her hand and spooned the spiced punch into a mug before adding a splash of rum. He heard his dad try to establish order in the living room, knowing it was an impossible task for even a high school principal.

"And..." Julia retrieved the spoon and set it on the plate Carlos scooted across the counter. Even with forty people milling around the house, his mother's kitchen was as tidy as the tiny woman with an oversized apron wrapped around her waist.

He leaned against the counter and sipped the spiced drink. "She's not ready for anything." He shifted uncomfortably under his mother's gaze. He'd known this conversation was going to happen the moment he'd casually mentioned inviting Sami and her kids to Christmas dinner.

"Do you want me to talk to her?" Julia unfolded her apron and lay it across the back of one of the four stools lining the counter high island in the middle of the kitchen.

Carlos shook his head. "I think it's a conflict of interest for you to treat her."

"It's not and I won't," Julia said. Carlos narrowed his eyes. Her tone was *too* casual. Having a psychiatrist for a mother came with pitfalls, one of which was her offers

27

to "help" her children with their love lives.

"I mean it, Mom. No talking."

She patted his cheek the way she had when she'd assured him she wouldn't have a little chat with the fourth grade bully who had made his life hell. She hadn't, she later reminded him, promised she wouldn't talk to the kid's parents. "Don't worry, *mijo.*"

Carlos sighed as she left the kitchen and studied the contents of his mug as if the key to Sami's heart lay in the diced apples and raisins floating on top.

"What's the sigh for?" He looked up as the object of his musings entered the kitchen, her cheeks flushed from the warmth of the living room and laughter in her eyes.

"What's going on out there?" he asked, ignoring her question.

"You didn't tell me there was an adult pinata," she said, holding up two small bottles of alcohol.

Carlos grinned. "Yeah, my dad started the tradition the year my cousin got a black eye from a three-year-old when he tried to steal her candy."

Sami laughed and set the bottles on the island.

"Are you having fun?" he asked her.

"I am," she said with a smile. "Thanks again for inviting me. Your family is..."

"Nuts?"

"I was going to say wonderful," she said softly.

"They're that too," he agreed, staring at her steadily.

Sami's eyes darted around the empty kitchen. Carlos knew she was uncomfortable being alone with him, but a part of him didn't care. "About dinner..." she started.

"Don't worry about it," he interrupted, draining his mug and setting it down.

"The thing is," she chewed her bottom lip.

"Seriously, Sami. Don't worry about it. It was weeks ago." Carlos pushed away from the counter. Irritation flared when she took a half step back. Patience, he thought to himself, didn't mean he couldn't be annoyed.

"I need to go see if Dad needs help." With what, he didn't know. He just knew he needed to get out of the kitchen and away from the woman who looked so right in his family's home.

He walked out of the room and into the chaos trying not to feel guilty over the hurt in her eyes.

❄

Sami carried Archie through the front door, his sleeping body limp in her arms. "Okay, you two. Bed," she whispered. She didn't get an argument as her two oldest shuffled their way to the bedroom the three shared. Penny crawled onto her bottom bunk fully dressed and closed her eyes. She was asleep in the seconds it took Sami to shift Archie in her arms and flick on the bedside lamp. Ben climbed to the top bunk, turning and sitting with his feet dangling over the edge.

"I'm too tired to take off my shoes."

"I got you, bud. Just give me a minute." Sami pulled back the covers on Archie's bed with one hand and lay him on the clean sheets. She pulled his shoes from his feet, wiggled his body out of his pants, and covered him up, tucking the blanket around his little body. She leaned down and kissed a cheek still crusted with cinnamon and sugar.

She walked to the bunk bed and took Ben's shoes off, letting them drop to the floor beside the ladder. "Did you have fun?"

"It was awesome," Ben said with a yawn. He tugged at his shirt. Sami climbed up a rung on the ladder and helped him take it off. "Carlos has the best family in the world."

"They're pretty fantastic," Sami agreed, climbing another rung as Ben crawled up the bed to his pillow, wiggling out of his pants. She took them from his fingers as he rolled over, his eyes closing before she'd had a chance to cover him. She pressed a kiss to her fingers and transferred it to his forehead.

Stepping down, she dropped his clothes next to Archie's pants. Lifting a sleeping Penny, she leaned her against her chest, holding her while she unbuttoned the back of her dress. Penny mumbled in her sleep, but didn't protest as Sami slid the dress of her, adding it to the growing pile on the floor. She tucked Penny under her covers, pressing her favorite stuffed rabbit next to her on the pillow.

She collected the pile of clothes and put them in the hamper, turned on the night light, and paused with her hands on the lamp switch.

She looked at her babies, all snug in their beds, their faces stained with ponche and churros and felt a lump rise in her throat. How she wished she could have them every Christmas. How she hated Franklin for tearing their family apart.

She turned off the light and walked into the silent living room. She didn't usually mind the quiet, but it was disjointing after spending the day with the warmth and noise of the Hernandez family.

She turned on her laptop, saw the Christmas messages from her mom and Franklin, and closed the screen again. She walked aimlessly to the tiny kitchen that would have fit in the laundry room of her old house and poured herself a glass of wine.

Her phone chimed as she took a sip of the petit syrah. Picking it up, she opened a message from Brie before dialing the Buchons' number. She didn't know what could be urgent on Christmas.

"Sami?" Brie's voice continued without pause, "I'm so sorry to call you this late, but I thought you might be home and we need a favor and I know it's Christmas." Brie took a breath. "Can you take Santiago for a couple days?"

Sami didn't think before saying, "Of course. When?"

"Now? Mark can be there in a few minutes."

"Now?" Sami ran through the mental list needed for housing a dog. Her landlord worked in animal rescue, so she knew that wasn't a problem, but, she looked at the clock, it was nearly midnight.

"The thing is," Brie's voice choked, "we've had a call from the adoption agency."

"Oh, Brie," Sami knew how desperately her friends wanted children.

"I'm trying not to get too excited," Brie whispered. "The situation is a little weird, but we need to go."

"I'm the last person to judge weird," Sami said with a laugh. "Bring him over." She disconnected the call and smiled as the clock changed to midnight, bringing Christmas - and her quiet evening - to an end.

❄

"Alone at last." Sami gave a crooked smile to Santiago. The dog's head tilted in acknowledgment while wide brown eyes stared steadily. "Well, come on, then." She walked over to the love seat positioned next to her Christmas tree and sat down, tucking her legs beneath her as she reached for a half-finished glass of wine.

It was late, too late to be up when she knew the kids would rise with the sun. She sipped the wine as Santiago lay his head on her lap. Absently, she rubbed the top of his head, her fingers playing in the rough fur while she stared at the ornaments decorating the tree. Green painted popsicle sticks formed frames around curling photos of a chubby-faced Ben. Glitter mixed with plaster caught the light as Penny's hand print twisted on its ribbon. Chunky beads filled a star shaped pipe cleaner, spelling out Archie's name. Franklin hadn't wanted any of the handmade ornaments, preferring to keep the crystal collectibles they'd decorated with before kids. She hadn't complained. Those bits of glue and paper and glitter were far more valuable to her.

Her phone chimed. She frowned and set down her glass. It was after midnight. Who could be texting this late?

You still up?

Sami's fingers hovered over the keypad while she re-read the three words. A month ago, she wouldn't have hesitated to reply to a text from Carlos, no matter how late he'd sent it. Things had been different since their date and tonight, during the only time she'd found to talk to him, things hadn't gone as well as she'd hoped. Santiago sighed loudly and set his head on the ground between his paws.

"You're right," she told the dog. "I'm being ridiculous." She thought for a moment, staring absently across the room. Santiago's tail thumped and something sparked a bit of mischief. She grinned and sent off a reply.

I am. Hanging out with a good looking guy and having a glass of wine.

Flirting had never come naturally to her. She'd met Franklin in college. Their relationship had been a whirlwind romance, flirting was unnecessary.

Anyone I know?

She smiled.

You know him. He comes into the restaurant sometimes. ;)

She snuggled into the pillows of the love seat and took another sip of wine.

Should I be jealous?

The butterflies in her stomach reminded her that there was an undercurrent that hadn't been there before their date, a sense that she was dangerously close to moving beyond playful flirting and into something more serious.

Nah. He's only here for a few days. He just needed a place to crash.

Sami waited for a reply, the clock ticking away the

seconds while the gray bubble appeared and disappeared.

Okay. Have fun.

Sami sat straight up, her mouth dropping open. "What?" Santiago lifted his head. "Have fun?" She looked at the dog in disbelief. "What does he mean by 'have fun'?" The dog rolled his eyes. "Exactly!" Sami said. She held up her phone and snapped a picture of Santiago, sending it with a terse, "*Will do.*"

She threw the phone down on the cushion next to her and picked up the wine again. *Have fun*? She fumed. Santiago sighed. "Don't take his side," she said sharply.

She picked up the phone and read over the short exchange, scrolling back over the weeks and then months. Years of messages rolled down the tiny screen. Sami stopped reading and let the words fly until she got to his first message.

This is Carlos. Got your number from Mark. Heard you need help moving. Let me know what time I need to be there.

Thanks! That is amazing. I can't pay much, but I appreciate it.

If you grab a pizza and beer, we'll call it good.

Sami read further.

I dropped off soup at your front door. Brie said you called in sick. Didn't want to wake you up if you were napping.

The man is an ass. I think you're beautiful.

How did your test go? I've got a bottle of wine with your name on it.

I have Saturday off. What time is Penny's soccer game?

She scrolled through movie dates, dinner plans, and pictures. Her hand shook as she put the phone down, gently this time. It was all spelled out in bubbles of blue and green. Years of building a friendship and under it all, more than simple kindness and companionship.

There was love.

She jumped at the sound of a soft knock on her door.

❄

She knew before she rose to her tiptoes and looked through the peephole who would be on the other side. She opened the door. "Hey."

Carlos stood on the dimly lit front porch, his hands stuffed into the pockets of the thick canvas jacket she'd helped him pick out. "Can I come in?"

"The kids are asleep," she whispered, holding the door open as he walked past her. Her body tingled with an awareness that, if she were honest, had always been there. She followed him into the living room where he prowled around the tiny perimeter, pausing to glance at pictures he'd seen dozens of times. His energy was contagious. She wished, for the first time, that the kids weren't at home so she could suggest a walk, a way to distract them from the conversation she knew they were about to have.

He stopped to pat Santiago absently on the head. The dog stretched and rolled to his back, the demand obvious. Carlos knelt next to the couch and rubbed the rangy mutt's stomach.

"Do you want something to drink?" Sami asked, wishing she could snag her glass from where it sat, inches from the man and dog.

Carlos shook his head. "I'd better not." He gave Santiago one last scratch and stood. "Look, Sami. You're right. We need to talk."

Sami crossed her arms in front of her, bracing herself for the emotional onslaught. She knew how these talks went. Hadn't Franklin had the same one with her? With a world shattering variation?

"I like you, Sami. A lot."

Sami nodded her head, not trusting herself to speak.

She waited for the but.

Carlos stepped towards her and set his hands on her arms, rubbing them gently. "Don't freak out on me."

"I'm not." Sami wanted to cringe at her tone.

"You are. Look. I can wait. It doesn't have to be now, but the thing is, I need to know if I even have a shot or if I'm wasting my time on something that isn't going to ever happen."

Sami closed her eyes. Silence blanketed the room, as she struggled with fears and old pain. Carlos's hands continued rubbing her arms, soft, soothing strokes anchoring her to the present. She opened her mouth, whispering the words her heart wanted her to speak. "I like you too. A lot."

"Tell me that with your eyes open."

Sami lifted her lids and looked into Carlos's warm brown eyes. "I like you too."

Carlos raised his eyebrows expectantly.

"A lot," she finished.

His face split into a smile, relaxing the lines of worry and stress she hadn't even realized were there. He pulled her to him, gripping her in a hug tight enough to make her ribs ache.

"But," she whispered into his neck, "I'm scared."

Carlos pulled back, unlocking her stiff arms and running his hands down to grip her fingers. "I'm scared, too."

Sami snorted. "You're young and hot," she flushed, "and I'm, well..." she pulled their hands to the side, exposing her body. "I'm not."

Carlos stepped closer until his chest touched hers and the air seemed to leave her lungs. He stared at her steadily. "I could kill that man for making you doubt yourself. Trust me. You are sexy as hell and I'm trying really hard not to kiss you senseless and drag you off to bed."

Sami's stomach dropped somewhere below where the

butterflies were fluttering. "The kids," she said, not caring that she sounded breathless.

"I know I can't do the second thing, but I think we're long overdue for the first." Leisurely, as if he was giving her time to back away if she wanted, he lowered his head. Sami closed her eyes and leaned toward him, giving in to the feelings she'd been trying to deny.

His lips were gentle on hers, moving across them with aching slowness. She felt tears prick her eyes at the love she felt behind the kiss. His lips eased insecurities and dimmed the years of begging for a crumb of affection. His thumbs rubbed her palm, the shaking of his arms telling her more than words that he wanted her. He pulled his head back and looked at her. "Okay?" he asked, his eyes scanning her face.

Sami took a breath, her heart hammering. "Oh, yeah," she said with a smile. She tugged on his hands, bringing him back down for another kiss. This one wasn't so gentle. He released her hands and wrapped his arms around her body, the muscles in his biceps flexing under her hands as she lifted her arms around his neck and let go of the past to hold tight to the future.

❄

Santiago stretched and yawned as the two humans kissed in front of the Christmas tree. He climbed off the couch and walked down the hallway toward the smell of sugar and children. He nuzzled the youngest one's face, cleaning his cheek with a quick lick. The little boy opened his eyes and with a sleepy smile moved over so Santiago could climb onto the bed. The youngest humans are my favorite, he told the angel checking on the children.

Don't discount the older ones, dog. They're all my favorites.

Santiago sighed as a little arm landed across his body.

His eyes closed to the vision of cream puffs as the angel disappeared. He knew there was more work to be done. After his nap.

AIRPORT CHRISTMAS
by Angela Amman

"Sugar, are you sure you need to fly home today?"

Margot wished she lived in a world where no one called her Sugar, but she didn't dare correct the owner of her favorite bed and breakfast. Nora had blown out eighty-three candles on her last birthday, and Margot felt certain she called every woman she met Sugar. The men, she'd learned, were generally Buddy or Bub, and the generic monikers were delivered with such sincerity Nora Lou was rarely corrected. She'd been christened Eleanor Louise but had been Nora Lou long enough that Eleanor seemed much too formal for the spitfire bed and breakfast owner who still insisted on making her own biscuits each morning, even though she'd hired a cook for just about everything else.

"Well, ma'am, I don't think you want to be cooking Christmas Eve dinner for just me," Margot said, gesturing around the echoing hallways of the cottage-like home. She'd first booked a room at the bed and breakfast while she was doing a training session four years before, after the conference center where she had a reservation egregiously double booked a third of their rooms. Staying at the Camellia Cottage made her teeth hurt with its quaintness, but she'd fallen in love with the little inn and never booked anywhere else when she swung through Charlotte for a training session.

"For you, Sugar, I'd bring out the fancy linens," Nora Lou winked.

Margot checked her phone one last time with a smile. Fancy linens seemed to be the only ones available at the Camellia, which was part of what she loved about it. Living in generic hotel rooms started sucking at her soul well over a year ago, and Nora Lou's hospitality offered a balm, if only for a few days at a time.

"I know you would," Margot said. "I can't imagine not being home on Christmas, though."

The lie felt almost like the truth. She'd repeated it over and over the last few days, and she wished desperately that she believed it. Reality wavered, of course, and she wasn't even sure the little apartment in Buffalo would feel like home when she got there. The last time she'd walked into the foyer several weeks ago, she hadn't recognized its scent. Since then, she'd been achingly lonely for something she couldn't define.

"Are you going to pull out that fancy planner of yours and book your next stay? I just can't believe we're welcoming in another new year."

"I don't think so, Nora Lou. I keep saying this is going to be my last training jaunt."

"Well then, Sugar. You get over here and give me a big squeeze. I'll miss seeing your smile around here," Nora Lou said.

Margot realized with a pang that the older woman's lilac talcum powdered hair smelled more like home than anything she could remember. "Maybe you'll bring that good looking husband of yours back for a weekend once you get things settled with the business."

Another one of Margot's lies hit her in the gut. She'd confided to Nora Lou that she was ready to sell the business she ran with her husband. She hadn't admitted she was alone in that sentiment.

"Maybe," she said, promising something she didn't know she could deliver.

"Oh my! I almost forgot!" Nora Lou reached up onto her tiptoes to retrieve a large mailer from the top of the old-fashioned apothecary cupboards behind the desk. "This arrived for you while you were out running this morning."

Margot's forehead furrowed. She hadn't requested any documents. An unfamiliar law firm's address shouted at her from the return address position, and her stomach plummeted. She'd been bracing herself for this package since her last fight with Vance, but in her worst nightmares, she hadn't expected to receive divorce papers the day before Christmas Eve.

Nora Lou always called the same car service, the driver smiling his recognition each time he hoisted Margot's shocking pink luggage into the trunk. Margot tossed her leather tote onto the seat next to her. The mailer stuck out from the top, and she covered it with her oversized cashmere wrap. The cranberry shawl kept her warm, hid wine stains after a turbulent flight, performed double duty as a pillow and blanket when needed, and now kept her from seeing something she couldn't stop thinking about.

"Miss Nora Lou thought you might not try to fly home today," Bert said. "I checked the weather myself, and looks like y'all are in for some major snow."

Each time he grinned at her in the rearview mirror, Margot smiled automatically, no matter what might be on her mind. Those gleaming white teeth in his perpetually tanned face couldn't be anything other than dentures, but the way his smile reached his eyes was the real deal.

"I can't imagine not being home for Christmas," she said, testing the mantra against the paperwork weighing heavily in her bag. The words felt just as true as before Nora Lou handed over the mail. She'd glanced at the weather in passing but wasn't concerned. Major snow didn't mean the same thing in Buffalo as it did down in Charlotte.

"Well, I understand that! We've been spending every Christmas since I can remember over at my mother-in-law's. It just wouldn't be the same without one of my wife's brothers drinking a little too much and wondering aloud why she married me," Bert said, chuckling at a joke he must have been telling for over half his life. She estimated his age somewhere well north of sixty.

"Something tells me if she hasn't regretted it by now," Margot said, pausing, "she's pretty likely planning to keep you around."

"I sure do hope so," he said. "So I understand why you'd want to be with your family at Christmas."

His words touched a nerve, bringing to mind one of the spokes of the always-circling wheel of the argument she and Vance had about selling their company. Margot folded her hands together to stop her fingers from making their way toward her mouth. She stopped biting her nails a few months after she started traveling around to do the training for the software Vance created moments after they finished business school. The habit crept back stealthily over the last six months. She meant to treat herself to a manicure at a salon near the conference center, but she'd been too exhausted to sink into any sort of chair except the one in front of Nora Lou's cozy communal table.

"Our families aren't really expecting us," Margot blurted. "We've both been traveling so much."

Bert's brow furrowed for a moment, working through the concept of a holiday not including a raucous family gathering, but he quickly recovered a thread of normalcy.

"I see," he said with a wink. "Just something special with you and your husband."

Margot dropped a wink of her own, then focused her gaze on the drop off lanes of traffic at the airport. Fewer cars than normal idled, which felt odd for the day before Christmas Eve. Bert hoisted her bag out of the trunk, and she tucked a larger-than-usual bill into his palm.

Anger rumbled in her gut, unexpectedly, and she yanked the package of legal paperwork out of her bag. Tossing it in the trash would be viciously satisfying but a waste of paper. Everything could — and would — be reprinted and redelivered. Instead she unzipped her suitcase and shoved it inside, not caring about her neatly packed bag.

Needing some sort of action to soothe her jumbled anger and sadness, she checked the bag. She thought she'd feel unburdened, but walking toward the security checkpoint without her trusted carry-on felt wrong, like she was leaving behind a part of herself. Maybe, she thought as she blinked away tears, she was.

❄

Vance Connelly juggled his phone and his coffee, knowing he should stash the device in his shoulder-slung messenger bag but trying to squeeze in one more email before he made it to the front of the baggage check line. His lips lifted into a rueful smile. His penchant for squeezing in one last anything — an email, a quick trip to a city where he'd almost closed a sale, a final drink before dinner shifted from business to fun — came up more and more frequently on Margot's list of things that made her think he'd never be ready to give up control of the company they'd built. A few drops of his caffeinated lifeline escaped the cardboard cup and trickled toward his Fair Isle sweater. Margot would have said he deserved it, but she would have rescued him from ruin by grabbing his cup and letting him finish the email with two free hands.

The smile drooped when he remembered how defeated her eyes looked during their last face-to-face chat. They'd always been the color of his favorite summer skies, her eyes, but in his memory they faded to something less, and he worried he'd been the one to change them. He dialed his attorney's number more in the last month than ever before, but he still wasn't sure how she'd react when she saw what he'd done. He shook his head. Even if it hurt, he knew he couldn't continue to pressure her into a life she clearly didn't want anymore.

By the time he made it to the counter, the email was finished, but another one caught his attention. He barely noticed the young woman behind the counter smiling shyly at him. With a name that sounded like a boy band member — and half the time, the perfectly tousled hair to match — Vance had grown used to the shy smiles of young women who were trying to place his face to a concert poster or some sidekick role in the latest rom-com.

"Just the one bag, sir?" Her name tag read "Holly," but he'd been through enough customer service lines to know she'd likely received at least fifteen saccharine comments about her seasonal moniker that morning.

"Yes, thanks. I don't normally check, you know? But I saw this gift I had to buy for my wife. We're in the middle of some upheaval, you could say, but she's still my wife, and, well, anyway, it wouldn't fit in my carry-on and..." He let his voice trail into the same nothingness as her tentative smile, which faded as soon as she heard the word "wife."

The rest of the transaction went quickly, and Vance finally put away his phone to rub at the headache forming at his temples. Why had he felt the need to share that he and Margot were fighting, especially in the middle of a line of people just wanting to get home for the holidays? He needed to buy aspirin before he got on the plane or he'd end up miserable by the time they were flying over Denver.

His brain, wired for calculations and the myriad of results each choice could have, knew he had a slight window of time before he might as well just order a double scotch and hope it would knock him out for the entire plane ride. He wanted to be awake when he got home, though. According to the tracking information forwarded from the attorney's office, Margot received the paperwork well before she left for the airport. By the time they both arrived in Buffalo, they were going to need to talk.

❄

Margot gave silent thanks to TSA prescreening, just as she did every time she bypassed snaking lines — and got to keep on her beloved riding boots. She couldn't imagine not traveling with them, especially as she made her way back to the snowy northern city she called home, but schlepping them in her luggage annoyed her. Of course, this time, her luggage rested in the belly of the plane, instead of awkwardly balancing in the overhead bins on the plane. Today, though, the lines were about equal — though she still got to keep on her shoes.

People stared at the monitors, but Margot tried not to worry about Bert's weather warning. Her flight to Buffalo still showed as on-time, though she noted an alarming number of incoming flights seemed to be canceling at rapid rates, especially those with departing cities in the northeast.

She pulled her phone from her bag, the instinct to message Vance as natural as breathing. They'd spent the past few years cobbling together their own private form of communication: texts, voice messages, and video calls all wove together to help them feel connected when they were generally traveling in opposite directions. Even now, with anger and hurt coursing through her body with each heartbeat, she couldn't disentangle herself from the knowledge he was in Los Angeles or the automatic calculating of time zones. She replaced the phone carefully, no longer sure how to speak to the man she loved.

"Where you headed, hon?" The question shook her out of her own thoughts.

The couple worrying at the oversized screen obviously weren't headed to Buffalo. Tropical flowers jumped off his shirt, and flamingos strutted across her neat shift dress. Margot idly wondered if she and Vance would spend retirement in coordinating clothes, before realizing she'd recently stashed papers into her suitcase that meant she and Vance weren't likely to ever worry about coordinating clothes again. Her mumbled answer to the polite query felt rude, but so did subjecting the unsuspecting couple to the tears threatening to fall.

Coffee would help. Coffee always helped. Even with smaller than normal crowds, the line at the coffee shop twisted outside of the kiosk. With her phone in her bag, she quickly felt its absence in her palm. She crossed and uncrossed her arms, unsure what to do without scrolling through social media or email.

"Going north?" The unexpected question caused her to stumble over her own answer. She would have thought years of travel and visiting countless new offices would have made her a little better at striking up random conversations.

"Yes. Buffalo," she finally said.

"No, really? Me, too!" the question-asker said.

He reminded her of Vance immediately. She sighed. With her husband swirling around in her head, of course any man with slightly shaggy blond hair and an easy smile would remind her of Vance. This stranger didn't really look much like Vance at all, with a bit of a beard and a battered fleece that looked like it actually saw its way around a hiking trail.

"Are you worried about the weather?" Margot asked. She wanted him to keep smiling at her, and the only way to do that was to keep talking.

"Nah," he said. "We're used to that, right?"

"Well, sure. But we're not the ones flying the plane," Margot said.

He grinned. "Not today, at least." His eyes trailed over the top of her head, and she realized she might have just lost his attention. "Your turn, I think."

Cheeks burning for thinking he might be flirting, she hurriedly ordered the biggest coffee she could and retreated to the closest bathroom. A quick glance in the bathroom mirror reminded her of one of her grandmother's favorite pieces of advice. She dug in her bag and took a minute to dig the tube of red lipstick from the bottom of her favorite makeup. Nothing seemed impossible while wearing red lipstick.

❄

Margot tucked her legs to one side and then the other, trying to figure out a way to get comfortable without infringing on her seatmate's right to legroom. Even with her slightly roomier economy-plus seat, there was no room for user error in the tight quarters.

Pulling out her book, phone, and earbuds, she settled back into the faux leather before remembering she'd definitely need her lip balm. They'd only boarded a few minutes earlier, and Margot had reached for her tote bag at least three times. The woman next to her couldn't have been sleeping already, and Margot's bustling wasn't exactly quiet, but her eyes remained stubbornly closed.

Spared from small talk, Margot ignored the safety lecture at the front of the plane and fell into the pages of a story she'd read on countless flights across the country. She liked the predictability of her favorite books and the way they surprised her with bits of whimsy and insight with each read.

Despite her determination to ignore reality, she couldn't stop the flood of thoughts racing through her head. Maybe she should have opened the mailer before shoving it aside. What did divorce papers look like anyway? And really, could Vance plan things any more poorly? Their recent conversations replayed over and over, in Technicolor, in her head.

About two months prior, she'd noticed a flurry of emails from an attorney before Vance changed the password on the joint account. His evasive answers about the emails, and the new password, exhausted her.

"We agreed to sell," Margot said.

"You remind me of that every single day," Vance replied.

"I told you eight months ago I only had six more months of this schedule left in me," Margot said. The ultimatum was almost impossible for her to deliver, and it stung when the date slid by without any sort of acknowledgment.

"I know, Margs. I do. And I want that for us, to spend more than a few days together each month. But I don't think it's time to stop the hustle quite yet." His smile, the one she knew he used at sales meetings, almost coaxed her into acquiescence.

"You'll never think it's time," she said.

"I will. You know I want to take things to a certain point and then sell when we've established it's a viable solution but —"

"But 'there's still room for growth'," Margot parroted his familiar words back to him. She couldn't help the sarcasm making her voice crueler than necessary.

"It's unfair to mock me. I've always been transparent about what I wanted for this project. Actually, these are goals we set together, years ago. I could say you're the one being unreasonable."

Her book open on her lap, Margot dug her fingernails into her palms. He'd been right, of course, but he'd been wrong, too. When they talked about running the small business on their own, they planned for a solid year of Vance selling the software and Margot training the businesses implementing it. Three years later, and Margot started to see her travel weariness wasn't hitting Vance nearly as hard. She let him know she only wanted to do the training for six more months, and she imagined him pulling away from her a little more each day as three seasons came and went without him mentioning putting out feelers for buyers.

"Excuse me, ma'am." A voice broke through the music she kept on as a way to deter plane conversations. The flight attendant stood at her elbow.

"I'll just have a water," Margot said, gesturing to the coffee still sitting half-full on her tray table.

"Actually, the gentleman offered to buy you a drink," the attendant said, nodding across the aisle.

"In that case, I'll have a red wine," she said.

Margot turned to see the blond hiker, not that she actually knew he was a hiker, sitting across the aisle and a few rows behind her. He grinned and shrugged. Margot wished he was sitting closer, so she could hear his warm voice again.

❄

The wine settled warmly in Margot's stomach, and she felt herself relaxing for the first time since sweet Nora Lou handed over the mail. She didn't even mind when her music slid into the soundtrack of a decidedly love-friendly Christmas movie and completely ignored the increasing turbulence shifting her tote bag back and forth at her feet. A tap on her shoulder shocked her out of her contentment cocoon, and only the smile greeting her from the seat behind her made the interruption slightly palatable.

"Do you believe in coincidences?"

"I don't know if coincidences are something to believe in," Margot said. "They just happen, don't they?"

"That's what I mean, though," he said. "Is it a coincidence that the seat behind you is empty? Fate?"

Margot cringed a little at the word. Fate never staked any claim in her belief system. One of the things cementing her attraction to Vance had been the way he laughed at the idea of destiny, insisting they were in charge of their own. Still, debating the machinations of the universe with an attractive stranger seemed to be the surest way to end the conversation.

"Maybe a little bit of both," she said, hedging her bets. Movement at the front of the plane caught her eye. The flight attendants clustered together, whispering.

"I'm Adam, by the way, and I don't normally do this," he said. "Buy wine for married women, I mean."

Margot's cheeks flamed into a shade of red matching the cranberry wrap she'd snugged around her arms. The sparkling rings on her left hand were so much a part of her existence she'd forgotten they broadcasted her marital status to the world. A flood of guilt washed on top of her embarrassment. How many times had she worried about Vance getting too friendly during his sales dinners? Now she welcomed a flirtation.

"And now I'm obviously sticking my foot directly into my mouth," he said.

"No. I appreciate the drink. I'm just having a day," Margot said.

"I can tell. I have a knack for that, believe it or not. I work with teenagers, and being able to tell when they're having bad days kind of goes with the territory."

"I'm not sure what it says about me that you somehow equated my emotional state to that of a teenager having a bad day," Margot said.

"Apparently I've also forgotten how to speak with adults," he said. "I just thought you looked you might need a gesture of kindness."

Margot was torn between the warmth of the intention and the sharp sting of realizing he hadn't been flirting with her after all. She took a deep breath, centering her thoughts. Until she'd seen his smile, she hadn't realized she'd missed that feeling of being bestowed with unexpected attention.

"I did," she said, forcing herself to stop over analyzing every word he said. "I'm Margot. Thank you for the wine."

The speaker system crackled to life above their heads. Margot instinctively gripped the armrest, though she remained twisted around in her seat, facing Adam.

"Thank you for your patience with the turbulence," the captain said. "Unfortunately the storms in the Northeast are more severe than we anticipated. We're diverting the plane for a landing at O'Hare."

More instructions droned overhead, but passenger chatter made them impossible to hear. Margot blissfully forgot all about the prior moments of embarrassment and blurted her frustration.

"Chicago? What are we supposed to do in Chicago?"

Adam shrugged a little. The nonchalance reminded her of Vance for the second time since she'd seen him in line for coffee.

"I don't know. Maybe they'll be able to get a plane off the ground later tonight."

"I doubt it," Margot grumbled. "And it's practically Christmas Eve."

"In that case," Adam said. "I'll let you return the favor and buy me a drink at one of the numerous airport bars Chicago has to offer."

❋

Vance's fingers flew across the keyboard of his sleek laptop. He never traveled without wi-fi, though it made him smile to think about how adamant Margot was about never working on a plane. His smile faded a little when he realized they wouldn't argue about their working habits any more.

The client he'd met with in Los Angeles was one of the first sales he ever made. Jack was shocked to hear Margot wouldn't be following in Vance's orbit in the New Year to train his new crew of payroll clerks.

"Half of why I work with you is knowing your pretty wife will be out here showing my girls how to operate that software," Jack said.

Vance cringed at the statement, but kept his mortification internal. He'd told Margot about Jack's unabashed sexism soon after he closed his first sale with the octogenarian. Margot sighed. *"You think it's surprising to hear someone talk like that, but you just don't notice because it doesn't affect you."* She trained Jack's team anyway, wryly briefing Vance each night about how Jack's twin daughters were essentially running the small furniture company Jack started years before they'd been born. In the early days, Vance reminisced, he and Margot communicated so frequently he could almost picture her training sessions.

He would miss those conversations.

The papers he'd sent to Margot weighed on his mind, and he closed his computer. Standing in the aisle for a moment to stretch his legs, he second-guessed the decision to have the paperwork delivered to the bed and breakfast. Margot raved about the Camellia Cottage, and he figured it would be almost like receiving the news at home. His head hurt when he calculated she probably spent just as many nights at the bed and breakfast as she had at their small apartment during the current year.

"Excuse me, sir, you're going to need to take your seat." The flight attendant's voice interrupted his thoughts, and immediately he noticed the strain she was attempting to veil with a smile.

"Of course," Vance said. He flipped open the computer again as the seatbelt sign flashed to life above his head. He didn't need to look at the information to know he and Margot were scheduled to arrive in Buffalo within minutes of each other. It would be the first time they were in the same city in well over a month, and he wondered why he'd thought it was a good idea not to wait until they were home to talk about the decision he'd made without consulting her.

Turbulence rattled the ice in the plastic cup sitting next to his laptop. He wished he would have ordered a single bourbon instead of a double, but the liquid was already sloshing in his stomach and slowing his thoughts.

"This doesn't feel right," Vance's seat mate said. Vance smiled automatically, preparing to smooth the panic he heard in the man's voice.

Another jolt of turbulence stopped him from assuring the man.

"I haven't been on a flight this rough for years," Vance said, letting countless flights scroll through his thoughts. He knew the weather in the Midwest and Northeast looked precarious for the evening, but he'd hoped they'd land before the snow got too heavy.

By the time the pilot announced they'd be grounding the plane far short of their destination, Vance closed his eyes against his pounding headache. He wished he would have waited to give Margot the papers in person. Now he wasn't even sure when he'd see her, and he knew she wouldn't check her own email before landing in Buffalo.

Maybe two bourbons had been one too few instead of one too many.

❄

By the time Margot and Adam were making small talk at a high-top table at a nondescript airport bar, she felt like she would either cry or scream if she heard one more person complain. A frantic woman barreled toward the bar, her dragged carryon bag careening off Margot's legs. She barked an order at the bartender and returned to loudly outlining the situation into a phone tucked beneath her chin.

"I know tomorrow's Christmas Eve, Mom! We had plenty of time to get to your house, but I can't make the planes fly into a blizzard," she said. "Yes, we're keeping an eye on the flights and maybe we'll get to you by tomorrow. Oh, Mom. This isn't Matt's fault. We agreed we weren't going to take the kids out of school early this year."

Despite her bruised shins, Margot sympathized, even more so when an equally frantic man and three young children tumbled into the bar and made a beeline for the woman. A pang of loneliness hit when she saw the couple's eyes meet. The woman handed her husband one of the two cocktails she'd ordered, and his rolled eyes seemed to release some of the tension in her shoulders.

"I can't think of much worse that being stranded in an airport with a bunch of kids," Adam said, sipping his beer as the family retreated to one of the tables in the corner. Backpacks and bags crowded together under the small table, but Margot thought the woman seemed at least a few degrees less frazzled since she'd been joined by her family.

"At least they're together," Margot said, ignoring the incessant vibration of her phone.

Adam laughed. "You might not think that in two

hours when the kids are asking for their third round of overpriced airport snacks and their parents have a splitting headache from cheap cocktails."

"Hey, you don't know they're drinking cheap cocktails," Margot said, unsure why she felt she should defend a family whose mother rammed a suitcase into her legs without so much as an apologetic smile.

"Trust me. No one flying coach with three kids is drinking expensive cocktails," Adam said. "When my ex and I used to travel with our son, we'd try to figure out how many of the cheap airport bottles of booze we could drink before one of us needed a nap."

Margot felt a little sting at the ease with which he mentioned an ex-wife and a son. She'd noticed the lack of a wedding ring when he'd commented on hers, but with her own concerns with her marriage at the forefront of her thoughts, she simply assumed unmarried bachelor. She felt a divorce should leave tendrils of shadow on one's self. Adam's easy demeanor didn't reflect any of the pain she'd been feeling the last few months.

"I've never flown with children," Margot said, mostly because she couldn't think of anything else to say. She resisted the urge to pick up her phone to check who'd been calling, fairly certain it was her mother, who managed to keep track of all of Margot's flights almost as well as Margot's infallible calendar system.

"But you fly a lot," Adam said, referencing her earlier description of her job.

"For now," Margot said.

"You mentioned that, but didn't elaborate," he said. "Are you getting out of the training business?"

Wine and low lighting loosened her tongue. "I'm getting out of the marriage business," she said.

"Really?" His raised eyebrows invited her to keep talking.

"Vance and I seem to have a difference of opinion about the lifestyle we want to lead," Margot said. "I don't think I can do this anymore."

"What do you think you'll do instead?" Adam asked.

Margot blinked, then stalled. "I wasn't aware I signed up for a career counseling session," she said.

"Well, I did mention I worked with high schoolers, right? Guidance counselors apparently don't take a Christmas break."

Scenes flashed through Margot's head. She'd been working the professional angles with Vance for so long that she could easily spout off sound bites about doing training for other companies or working with conference centers to set up professional conventions. Truly, though, she'd pictured their lives after selling the company from a more personal angle: lazy weekends checking out wineries along the Niagara, a little boy with Vance's shock of blond hair, dinners that didn't come from a room service cart.

Ending her life with Vance meant the end of the company, which was a relief, but it meant the end of those dreams, too.

"I'm not exactly sure what I'll do next," Margot said. Needing something to do with her hands, she picked up her phone and scrolled through the missed texts. Blood drained from her wine-flushed cheeks.

"Is everything ok?" Adam asked.

"It's just that Vance is here. In the airport. His plane got diverted, too."

❄

Margot took a shallow breath and tested the idea in her brain: Vance was here, wandering the terminal, close enough they could crash into one another like a romantic movie. A deeper breath and she might be able to wrap her head around it. Despite the way she'd been feeling about him for the past few hours — maybe the past few months if she was being honest — Margot felt relief flood her veins. Her fingers flew over her keyboard to let him know how to find her in the terminal bar.

Everything always seemed less dire with Vance at her side, from road tripping to a bowl game their senior year to starting a business they had few qualifications to start. Even this ill-timed Chicago detour could be more like an adventure, at least it could if she forgot about the papers in the belly of the plane sullenly sitting at the gate.

Adam shrugged, his smile showing the dimples she'd noticed while standing in line for coffee, a line that seemed to exist days in her past instead of mere hours. "I guess this makes me extra baggage."

"No! Stay. We can all have dinner together," Margot said, though she could hear the distraction in her voice as she dug through her bag to find the red lipstick she'd already turned to once that day for a boost of confidence.

"This is why married women are bad news," he teased. "Husbands always seem to show up when you least expect them."

"That's not the only reason you should stay away from them," she said. "Seriously, though, don't feel like you have to disappear. Who knows how long we'll be here. Besides, Vance and I are in the middle of...well...it's complicated." She cringed, wondering if she only wanted Adam to stay to let Vance know she wasn't completely invisible to other men.

"No offense, Margot," he began, his grin turning into a grimace at her words.

Margot prepared herself to be offended, as she always did when someone prefaced a comment in such a way. "I've enjoyed chatting with you, but if I wanted to be in the middle of complicated marital situation, I would've just stayed married."

Margot's heart stuttered at his words. Part of her savagely wished he never sent her over a bottle of airplane wine. Her emotions were all over the place without offhand commentary from an attractive man who made divorce sound like an attractive option. Not to mention, having him quickly gulp down his beer and collect his backpack made her feel like she'd been engaged in something elicit rather than simply passing time during an unexpected situation.

She opened her mouth to try to explain her remark further, then snapped it shut. She'd spent over a year trying to explain and justify her feelings to her own husband with disastrous results. She didn't owe anything to this stranger except the beer she'd promised him, no matter how charming he might be.

"Thank you for keeping me company," she said instead, and the simple statement of gratitude coaxed genuine smiles out of them both.

"No problem," he said. "Good luck with the complications, and fingers crossed I see you on a flight later tonight."

Before she could respond, his eyes shifted to a place over her shoulder. Margot didn't have to swivel in her seat to know what happened. She could smell Vance's soap mingle with the overheated, fried food-infused airport air. She would recognize it anywhere, the soap she started buying for him well before she knew she'd marry him,

His hand on her shoulder felt like home, yet surreal, and the hurt in his voice made her dizzy.

"Well, I can't say this is how I pictured our unplanned reunion."

❉

Vance saw confusion in Margot's eyes when she turned in her seat, but he couldn't see guilt lurking there. In his gut he knew she wasn't squirreling away time with the scruffy interloper skulking away from the table, but it felt surreal to see his wife sitting and having a drink with another man.

He tried to smile, shrugging in a way that felt wrong. "I thought we'd have more of a 'run into my arms' kind of moment," he said.

Her eyebrows arched into her hairline.

He tried again. Apologies didn't come easily, even when he wanted them to. "I guess it just looked differently in my head."

"I know the feeling," Margot said, and he tried to wrap his head around the weariness in her voice.

"Let's start over," he said, still unsure why she was looking at him like he might vanish into thin air. "Since fate threw us together when we were supposed to be apart, can I buy you a drink?"

"Fate apparently has a sense of humor," Margot said.

Vance knew every nuance of her voice, could read them in her text messages and emails and the exhausted calls they squeezed in when they were on opposite sides of the country. He hadn't expected to hear hurt and resignation in her voice when he realized they were both sidetracked in Chicago. Once upon a time, they would have looked at the coincidence as an adventure. Had they really grown so distant? And what did that mean for the papers his lawyer put together so carefully?

He dropped his bag at her feet and pulled the chair closer to hers before sitting. He'd been traveling long enough that his head throbbed from lack of sleep and the dehydration creeping through his body. Habit allowed him to reach for her water glass and gulp more than half of it down before she could protest. Relief crackled in his veins when he saw her smile a fraction of an inch.

"You never think about ordering your own water, do you?" Her words echoed with nostalgia, which confused him, but he grasped at the small victory turning up the corners of her mouth.

"I didn't even order our drinks yet," Vance said, smiling back. "You can't get mad about the water."

He could see her struggling to hold back tears, and he

reached down to grab her hands. "Margs. Did something happen? I thought this would be fun. Or at least as fun as a severe weather delay can possibly be."

"Yesterday, I would have thought that, too," she said, and his heart stuttered as her voice caught somewhere in her throat "But then you served me with papers, and I don't know what to think anymore. And in a hotel? I don't know. Maybe it's better it happened there than at home..."

Vance felt torn between gathering her to his chest and trying to make sense of what she was saying. She'd seemed so unhappy for so long. She should have welcomed the news, even if she was initially surprised, but now she was near tears over it. His head swam. He drained her glass of water, wishing he could somehow start this whole conversation over again.

"What do you mean? I thought you'd want to know as soon as possible," Vance said.

She pulled her hands back into her own lap, eyes wide with pain. "I just... I knew we were struggling to get back on the same path, but I never thought you'd be this cavalier about getting divorced."

Vance's tired brain felt pieces click into place, and he might have started to laugh if Margot's eyes weren't swimming with tears.

"Margot, did you even open the damn package?"

❄

Margot's gut twisted at Vance's exasperation. Ever since she'd seen his eyes, she hadn't been able to keep up with her conflicting emotions, let alone the way his mood bounced all over the place. His hands warmed hers when he grabbed them, just like they had so many times since they first linked fingers in the chilly Buffalo air.

"I didn't read through everything," she said. "I was leaving for the airport by the time I got it, and then I just didn't feel like dealing with them in public."

She couldn't understand why he was smiling.

"Well, could you take a minute and open them now?" he asked. "Maybe I should have done it this way in the first place, waited until we were together."

"They're in my bag. My checked bag," she said.

He laughed. "Of course they are. Since when do you check a —? Never mind. I guess it doesn't matter."

"What do you mean it doesn't matter?" Margot asked. "I think it matters! Our lives are completely changing."

"Well, yes," Vance said. "But not the way you..."

"Margs," he started again, reaching for her hands. "I didn't send you divorce papers. I sent you the papers for the sale of the company."

Margot felt all the blood in her body drop into her chest and then climb back into her face. Flaming red with embarrassment, she started to piece together what happened. How could she have actually believed Vance would send over divorce papers by mail? She would have buried her face into her hands if they weren't still clasped in her husband's.

"The sale..." Her voice failed her.

"Yes! I finally found a buyer I thought made sense for us, and I had the papers drawn up as a kind of holiday surprise. You'll need to sign off, of course, but since you've been talking about this for so long, I figured you'd be thrilled."

"I would be. I am."

"I also kind of figured you'd open the envelope and not assume I wanted to divorce you," Vance said.

Margot felt her face get even hotter, though she hadn't thought that was possible a moment before. "I can't believe I thought that. Oh God, Vance, are you livid?"

She could see the combination of laughter and relief in his eyes as he pulled her off the chair and into his embrace. He held her face in his hands and kissed her, neither of them caring about the close quarters of the quickly crowding airport bar.

"I'm just still shocked that we could get tangled up in this kind of misunderstanding after everything else we've navigated together," he said. "I mean, we run a pretty successful business."

"Ran. We ran a very successful business," she said.

"You haven't signed anything yet," he teased.

"I'd sign them right now if they weren't buried in a plane somewhere," she said. "Are you sure, though?"

"Of course," he said, his lips pressing into her hair. "I let them know we'll be available to consult for six months, but anything they need from us has to be addressed in New York."

Margot pressed her forehead against his chest and breathed him in for a minute before leaning back to look into his face. She saw the certainty in his eyes and knew he was at peace with his decision.

"But what are we going to do?" She asked.

"I thought you'd have that planned," Vance said, laughing.

"Part of me didn't think you'd ever sell," Margot admitted. "So I guess I didn't have much of a plan."

"Well," Vance smiled. "I actually have a seed of an idea, but I'm not sure how you're going to feel about it."

❊

Margot spread her hands on the table in front of her, eyes resting on her wedding ring with a goofy grin glued to her face. Vance followed her eyes and traced the band with his finger.

"I guess I should be glad you didn't toss this in the Mississippi, huh?"

"Don't be melodramatic," Margot said, still smiling, "I would have sold it and traveled the world."

"Speaking of," Vance started, his brow furrowed as

he clicked around the phone nestled in his palm, "I don't think we're going to be flying out of here tonight."

Margot didn't bother to confirm his words. Emotional whiplash should have rendered her exhausted, but Vance's news held the promise of a future she hadn't been sure she believed in any longer. Adrenaline and contentment battled in her brain, but though she couldn't stifle her yawn, she couldn't imagine falling asleep either.

"Christmas in Chicago?" she asked. They'd been to the city in another lifetime, back before they flew across the country more frequently than they spent time at home.

"Maybe," Vance said.

Margot recognized the noncommittal tone. "Or?"

"Well, I know we're expected home at some point," Vance said.

"Some point like tomorrow," Margot said. "Some point like Christmas Eve and then Christmas, remember?"

"I know," Vance said.

"But?"

"Well, you asked what we were going to do, and I've actually been thinking about it a lot," he said.

She wasn't sure if she wanted to hear how he imagined their lives could look.

"Do you remember Josh?" Vance asked.

"CPA Josh or cage fighter Josh?" Margot asked.

"CPA Josh," Vance said. "Though I'm pretty sure cage fighter Josh gave that up about three years ago and went to the police academy in Atlanta."

"So, why do I need to remember CPA Josh? Didn't he disappear into some little town upstate?"

"Not exactly. Little town, yes. But it's not too far from our place, actually. Drivable, for sure. On the water."

The ease with which he spoke of their little apartment

settled comfortably in her chest. "And Josh has something to do with what you want to do next?"

"He wants to open a finance firm. Small. Maybe firm isn't even the right word. But he wants to help local businesses manage their money, and he needs help. He's good with numbers, better than anyone I know, actually. But he's helpless with all the rest of it, the tech, the promotion, the daily running of a business."

"And we can do that," Margot said. "We're kind of fantastic at that."

"We are, indeed, fantastic at that."

"We'd have to leave Buffalo?"

"It's an hour away, I think. We can map it out. Maybe we could commute for a while," Vance said.

Margot thought about their apartment. She could barely picture what they'd put on the walls. The only thing she could conjure was the smell carried on Vance's hair.

"Or maybe we could try something new," she said, reaching to bury her face in his neck.

Vance's eyes brightened. "I don't want to make a decision without weighing all our options. But I had this idea maybe we should ditch the return flight and rent a car and drive over to this little town and see how they do Christmas."

Surprising herself, Margot smiled and laced her fingers through Vance's. "Let's do it."

"Really?" He asked, and for the first time in countless long months, she felt her stomach flip with excitement about the future.

"I think," she said, slowly, "if we're together, anywhere might feel like home."

THE SOLOIST
by Cameron D. Garriepy

Hank, whose neon-illuminated name graced the roof of the dining car on Washington Street, lost track of the purchase order he was tallying when he heard an angel singing in the alley behind the diner.

O come all ye faithful, the angel instructed, *joyful and triumphant.*

It was a fearless voice, deep and ringing, pure and low, with an ease about it. This angel loved to sing and her joy burst through the walls despite the pre-dawn hour. Hank abandoned the books and pushed through the swinging door to the kitchen to investigate just as the angel let herself right in through the delivery door.

She broke off just as *Come and behold Him* rose high in her register, the truncated note ringing around the tiny kitchen like a living thing. "I'm sorry." She laughed like a big church bell. "I forgot to knock."

The angel was near six feet tall, in a yellow quilted parka and a sky blue ski hat. She stuck out a broad hand with short, clean nails. "Talia Benson, your new cook."

Hank recognized her speaking voice from their brief phone interview the day before. He'd been so desperate to get a cook into the kitchen, he'd hired her unseen. Handshake dispensed, she shrugged out of her jacket. His wife Gayle would call Talia Benson a handsome woman, he thought. The phrase *brick shithouse* also came to mind. "Pleased to meet you. We open in an hour. Menu's taped over the griddle. Can you make coffee?"

"Like my Mama never could." Talia smiled wide and Hank found the corners of his mouth rising too. "I'll get settled in and get a pot on."

She revealed a head full of spiky orange hair when she pulled the hat off and jammed it into the sleeve of the parka.

Hank left her to figure things out, and she wasted no time. The vent hood kicked on, and in short order the satisfying perfume of hot griddle and strong coffee wafted out from the kitchen. Hank forgot to turn on the FM radio he kept by the register; Talia was a one-woman Christmas songbook. That voice soared over the clanking and sizzling from the kitchen and Hank was hard pressed not to sing along when she got to *Let It Snow*.

❄

The last hour before opening ticked away, and five AM meant two things at Hank's Washington Street Diner: Hank would flip the sign and unlock the front door, and Pastor Hunt would be waiting outside for coffee and an egg-and-sausage biscuit.

"Mornin', Hank." Reilly Hunt kicked the door frame to knock gray slush from his boot treads before stepping inside. He chafed his hands together and unzipped his coat.

"Mornin', Reilly." Hank tossed a copy of the Gazette on the counter at the pastor's usual seat, and called back to the kitchen. "Number six!"

Talia's voice rose up over butter hitting the hot grill in a rich run of *Gloria, Hosanna in excelcis!*

Reilly peered through the service window without luck. "You hiding an opera singer back there?"

Hank set a mug of coffee down in front of the town's favorite spiritual leader. "About as likely as anything else she might be."

❉

Reilly parked his truck in the old barn behind the church. At seventeen, the old Ford didn't owe him anything, and Reilly knew it. He skipped his jacket; the heat in the truck only had two settings: Off and Death Valley. Sure, the sweat might freeze in his hair, but the cold air was welcome after the ride in from his house outside town.

"Jojo?" He called out into the still, cool air of the empty hall.

He was answered by a deafening G-major chord from the organ. "Back here!"

The church's administrative assistant, who also played the organ, taught Sunday School, and led the choir and weekly Bible study, popped out from behind the organ. Reilly knew she was somewhere in her forties—she'd only been a few years ahead of him in school, but you'd never know it. Jojo's face was young, as was her heart. She dressed in long skirts and combat boots or short skirts and jeans together; her inky black hair was pixie short. Her skin was a vibrant living canvas, and no amount of *tsk-ing* from his older congregants could convince her that a nose ring was unseemly.

"I was looking to see if I'd left Jesus in the cubby last year."

Reilly couldn't help laughing. "You don't carry Him always in your heart?"

Jojo set her hands on her hips and gave him the stink eye. "The baby. For the Nativity. I can't find him with the others."

"Did you look in the office supply closet? Millie helped us clean up last January..." Jojo's nod was understanding. "How was practice?"

He'd deliberately waited until after choir practice to come by and set up the Fraser fir he'd bought for the annual gifting tree. No fewer than four members of the soprano section were actively pursuing him - for themselves or for their daughters.

"Bad news," Jojo said, nudging a box of lights and garland toward the tree stand. "Nancy Elder's daughter in Seattle went into labor early. She and Sid leave in the morning and Nance says they'll stay through the New Year. We just lost our soloist."

Reilly considered. For twenty-five years, Nancy Elder had guided the good Congregationalists of town through two Christmas Eve services with a clear, light soprano and a natural instinct for performing. This was a setback, but nothing beyond their mortal scope. Jojo was watching him, waiting for a call to action. He grinned at her.

"He will deliver."

Jojo hoisted a coil of lights and began to untangle them. "I sincerely hope He delivers an opera singer pronto, Doc."

Reilly considered again. This time, it was the excellent breakfast sandwich and coffee at Hank's. And the hidden voice he'd delighted in while he ate. He had a homily to write, the baby Jesus to find, and a shift at the food pantry, but he could drop in at Hank's before the diner closed and introduce himself to the mysterious singer.

He just might have delivered already.

❄

Hank's was never empty unless it was closed, but Reilly rarely saw the afternoon crowd. His arrival was met with pleasant, but frank curiosity. For every nod, every *hey Doc*, every smile, there was a question. *What's he doing here at this time of day?* They were—as was he—creatures of habit.

Creatures who sat quietly over coffee, pie, or sandwiches; quietly because they were listening to that voice. He paused to drink in the way she navigated *We Three Kings of Orient Are*, the kitchen noise her percussion. Surely whoever she was, she couldn't be unaware of the effect her voice had on the patrons?

"Afternoon, Reilly." Hank motioned to an empty corner table by the front windows. "I've got that table, but your spot's taken."

"I'm not here for biscuits. I'm here—" The singer swooped into the chorus and Reilly's skin tingled. "Has she been singing all day?

Hank's smile was wistful, bordering on foolish. "She hummed for a while, but mostly, yeah."

"Can I go back?"

Hank set down a plated meatloaf sandwich. "I'll introduce you."

Reilly followed Hank through the swinging door. She was washing dishes, humming over the steaming water in the vast sink. She was... a knockout.

Hank rapped lightly on the counter. "Talia?"

"Yeah, Hank?" She stopped humming, looked up, and blinked at Reilly. "Oh, hi."

Her eyes were fiery blue. Reilly rocked back on his heels to take the full magnificent height of her. "Hi."

Hank took over the introductions. "Talia Benson, the Reverend Doctor Reilly Hunt, pastor at the Grove Street Church. Reilly, Talia's my new cook. Fresh off the bus from... Where'd you say you were from?"

"I didn't." Talia's mouth tipped at the corners— Reilly wouldn't have called it a smile—and she dried her hands. "Pleasure to meet you, Reverend."

"I've gotta head back out front," Hank said, returning to the register, where a short queue was forming. "Holler if you need me."

An awkward silence threatened, so Reilly filled it. "Call me Reilly."

"Reilly." Talia took off a worn Boston Red Sox cap. She had carrot-red hair worn in a short, choppy cut that emphasized a long neck and strong cheekbones. "Is this an official visit to save my soul?"

Reilly heard a wariness in her question, though her tone was light. "Official visit, yes. Your soul is your own. You have a beautiful voice, Ms. Benson."

"Talia." She corrected him with a blush. "Thank you. Sometimes I forget people can hear me."

"Lucky us."

She laughed at that. Her laugh was like a timpani roll. "You say that now."

"I can't imagine saying differently." Reilly leaned against the door to the walk-in refrigerator. "You've got a gift."

Those blue eyes narrowed fast. "What can I do for you, Reilly?"

Reilly felt that gaze pierce his chest. Here was a woman who didn't trust flattery. Best to come out with it then. "Sing with our choir. On Christmas Eve. We need a soloist."

"No." Her answer was so swift and decisive Reilly wasn't sure he'd heard her correctly. She seemed to catch herself as well. "I'm sorry. But no. I'm sure you mean it as a compliment, but I can't."

"Ms. Benson. Talia." He'd seen a flash of hurt in her eyes. He'd hurt her somehow. Or bought up an old hurt. The desire to make it right sucker-punched him. He reached out, as if to comfort her, but stopped just in time to save himself more embarrassment.

She snugged the cap back down over her hair and

turned back to the sink. "I appreciate you coming by, Reverend, but I should get back to work."

※

Talia came home to a cold, dark house. There was grease in her pores, and her feet ached, but she had a day's pay in her purse and hope in her pocket.

She deposited a to-go cup of coffee from Hank's and a bag of pantry staples from the market next door on the chipped formica table that came with the rental. Her phone chimed—a text from Eli—and Butter, their rescue mutt, padded in from the back of the house. He yawned, stretched, and moved to sit by the door, his brindled backside sliding a little on the faded welcome mat.

"Your boy's on his way home from somewhere. He'll take you for a proper walk later." Talia jingled his leash. "This is just to pee."

Butter, so named because his first act as a member of the family had been to eat a full stick of the stuff right off the counter—wrapper and all–tugged in the direction of the sidewalk, but Talia pulled him back toward the door. The wind was up, and the cold had teeth.

Inside, she started the water in the shower, cranking the water temperature up to scald away the smell of diner food. She nearly screamed when she tripped over a baby doll on the floor in front of the toilet. *How the hell had that thing gotten in the house?* When her stomach returned to its usual spot, she bent to retrieve the toy from the floor. Butter had definitely loved on it some. There were distinct canine teeth-marks on the doll's chubby elbows, and one foot was shiny with dog drool.

She opened the bathroom door to find Butter waiting for her, tongue lolling and tail wagging. "Where'd you find this treasure, hmm?"

Butter sat, watching the doll with adoring eyes while Talia inspected it. Other than the initials G.S.C. Sharpied on the bottom of one foot, it was a small, unremarkable doll. Another text from Eli pinged. *Lost track of time. Home soon.*

She closed the bathroom door in Butter's face. "I'll see you after my shower, tough guy."

Under the hot water, it was easy to dwell on the preacher's face when she shot him down. He defied every image of a cleric she'd ever considered, with his outdoorsy clothes, and his scruffy, handsome face. She wondered how the preacher's wife felt about the sparkle she'd caught in his eye when he first saw her. That admiration had warmed her right through, until he'd revealed that he wanted something from her.

They always wanted something from her.

The dog was nowhere to be seen when Talia got out of the shower, so she wrapped herself in a towel and went to find some clean clothes. The kitchen door slammed, followed by pounding feet and the flush of the toilet. Talia smiled to herself. Eli mostly favored her, long boned and broad featured, but he had his father's coloring. She pictured his dark hair falling over one eye while he washed his hands, and hoped that coloring was all he'd taken from his paternal gene pool.

She wasn't prepared for the second door slam.

"Eli?"

When he didn't answer, she swung through the bathroom to grab the doll, then knocked on his bedroom door. The house still felt like someone else's, as though she were knocking on a stranger's door, but they'd done this enough times that she knew they'd settle. A week wasn't very long to make a house feel like home.

"Yeah." She could hear the foul humor in his voice.

With a deep breath, she nudged open his door. Her thirteen year old son took one look at her, paused in his doorway in her yoga pants, oversized sweatshirt, and hair towel, holding a baby doll, and said quite succinctly, "Oh, shit."

✳

Reilly finished printing requests and recipient numbers on the Gifting Tree tags somewhere between two and three in the morning. He yawned, set his desk back in order and left the pile of tags on Jojo's desk for the morning. The need in the community broke his heart every year, but it was always mended when the congregation provided. On the way out to the barn to warm up the truck, he went through his mental checklist. There was one last Advent Sunday sermon to write, the baby for the Nativity to locate, a soloist to find…

He sat in the cab of the truck, watching the stars and thinking of Talia Benson. She wasn't what anyone would call his type—if he had one—but there she was, occupying valuable real estate in his head. A beautiful voice, joy in the singing, engaging and vulnerable all at once. A mystery. And then there was his physical reaction to her. She was…striking. Reilly believed wholly that there were forces greater than himself at work in the world; he sensed that Talia was going to teach him something, but life, and God, had a way of throwing curveballs.

He swung the truck out onto the rural route where his parents' place—he'd never been able to call it his, though it had been his since they left for Arizona— huddled near the State Forest tree line. The sky was infinite, the stars dizzying and brilliant, as he rumbled along past a small clutch of cottages that passed for a neighborhood that far from town.

It seemed his lessons didn't observe daylight hours, for there she was, Talia Benson sitting on the stoop of Jerry Griffin's rental under the yellow light of a bare exterior bulb. He couldn't read her expression in the deep shadows, but he knew the bend of world-weary shoulders. He glanced at the dashboard clock with a sigh and eased the truck onto the shoulder.

Rolling down the window, he called softly. "Ms. Benson? Talia? You okay?"

She looked up and Reilly noticed a mug between her clasped hands. "Depends on who's asking. And why."

"A concerned neighbor," he offered, letting the truck idle and making no move to leave the cab. He held still while she contemplated him.

"I wouldn't mind some company." The admission sounded defeated. "Do you do this a lot?"

Drop in on an intriguing, frustrating stranger in the small hours of the morning? "I can't say that I do."

He turned the key and left it in the ignition, grabbed a hat and mittens, lovingly if not tidily knitted by Jojo, and suited up for the cold. Talia was wearing shapeless shearling boots, and a parka over a sweatshirt, the hood pulled up to cover her bright hair. His lungs pinched, not from the cold, but from the sense of *rightness* about crossing the small yard in the starlight to comfort her.

He sat two steps below her, keeping as little of his rear end on the cold stoop as possible. "It's late. And cold."

She snorted. It was unladylike and delightful. "Did you master the obvious in divinity school, or do you come by it naturally?"

"Strictly a product of my upbringing," he countered. "And it's been a long day."

Talia toasted him with her mug. "It really has. I'm tired of my problems. Tell me about yours."

"Well," he leaned his head against the cold railing and closed his eyes, "I spent the morning in the city, there's an at-risk youth program I volunteer with. Holidays can be hard. The afternoon was mostly what passes for hard labor in my profession. This coming Sunday's the last one before Christmas Eve, which means folks expect some garlands and wreaths, and I hate ladders."

Her voice was soft. "Me, too."

74

Reilly could feel sleepiness rising up from his belly; the hour was finally catching up with him, but so too was a promising weight in the air between them. "And Jojo's in a panic over Jesus—"

Talia cut him off. "Who's Jojo?"

"The church's Girl Friday, for lack of an official title." Reilly shrugged. "So we spent some time looking for Him."

"Like actually looking? As opposed to... searching?"

Reilly opened his eyes to find her looking hard at him, a touch of laughter in her eyes. He chuckled, opening up to her humor. "Millie Silver put it away last year, and we can't find it. Jojo's in a tizzy—"

"Did you just say, 'tizzy?'" Talia's laugh let fly. *Timpani*, he thought again. *Steady, booming.*

"Anyway, the baby doll is missing..."

Talia's laughter stopped like she'd turned off the tap. The wariness was back. He didn't know what wrong things he'd said, but he couldn't help the happy thrill of connection they'd shared before he'd said them.

"I should go in," she said, rising. "You're not too far from home?"

"Nope." Reilly took the hint. "Goodnight, Talia."

✳

A woman's only day off in a week wasn't meant to start with hauling her son to church by his ear. Not literally by his ear, and not to church—in that sense, but to the church. The handsome, kind Reverend Doctor Reilly Hunt's church.

If ever there was a man she shouldn't have gone to bed dreaming about kissing, he was that one. Nonetheless, she'd crawled into the bed in the bedroom she'd yet to really nest in imagining a version of the night that ended with his lips on hers, his hands—not as soft as you'd imagine a preacher's hands to be—on her face, her neck. Her body.

It didn't matter to her body that ultimately he was after her voice and her service to his congregation. His kindness in the dark of night seemed genuine enough. A perk of his career, she supposed.

And there was still the question of a wife. *Didn't small town reverends have wives? Children?*

They approached the side door of the church, where a charming sign directed visitors to the office, and Talia shook off impure thoughts of the pastor. Eli trudged sullenly behind her carrying the baby doll in a paper grocery bag; his shame keeping time with his shadow in the late-morning sun.

The office stood empty, but a familiar melody swirled through from the hall. Someone, two someones, she realized, were playing *Silent Night* on piano and guitar. She held them both back in the doorway. Reilly and a fine-boned woman with vast and intricate tattoos visible up her arms were playing the duet, illuminated by a clear bar of light from the vaulted window over the front door. For a moment, the worry of their errand vied with hot jealousy in her belly.

Dust-motes danced around the pair while them while Reilly strummed and the woman's fingers danced on the worn piano keys; as it always did, the music eased her heart.

Eli was always telling her she was singing when she hadn't been aware of doing it, so when Reilly looked up, and the piano harmonies faded, Talia caught herself, flushing scarlet and snapping her mouth closed.

"You know the German?" A grin a mile wide spread on the woman's face.

"Only the first verse," Talia stammered.

The woman stood. She wore combat boots and thick wool socks, a huge fisherman's sweater over patterned leggings, and a silver hoop though her nose. *That's the haircut I was trying for*, Talia thought.

"Johanna Moretz." The woman stuck out a hand. "But everyone calls me Jojo. Tell me you're planning on auditioning for our choir? Please."

Reilly must have seen the distress on her face. He interrupted, concern thickening his voice. "What brings you here, Talia?"

She pulled Eli in front of her, planting him between the reverend and herself. "My son has something to say."

"Son?" Reilly phrased it as a prompt, but Talia couldn't help hearing it as a judgment.

"This belongs to you, sir." She heard the squeak in Eli's voice, a brutal reminder that he was on a cusp. That she had to stay vigilant.

Reilly rose, still holding the guitar, to take the bag Eli thrust out. He peered inside. "Where'd you come by this?"

Eli muttered something that sounded like it ended in, "Dare." Talia squeezed his shoulder.

Her son lifted his chin and stared down the pastor. "Some kids from my homeroom were gonna take it on Christmas morning. I told them their plan was shitty... sorry, sir... Crappy, and they were gonna get caught. I was showing off, trying to get them to like me. Sucks being new all the time. So... one of them... told me where to find it, and I snuck in here and took it." His defiance deflated visibly, then he stared at his feet. "I was going to bring it back."

Silently, Reilly handed the bag to Jojo, who whisked it away into the back entryway. Reilly set down his guitar and drew in a deep breath. "Eli, do you think it's fair of me to ask that you help Jojo and me some around the church, by way of apology?"

Eli nodded assent without looking up, and the hard knot in Talia's chest loosened.

Reilly looked over Eli's head at Talia. "Maybe he takes the school bus out here next week after school, helps out until you can come pick him up?"

Talia nodded, blinking back the stinging threat of tears. "That sounds okay to me. Generous, even."

"Maybe you both come to Sunday service? Eli can help Jojo get set up… and you'd get a chance to meet your neighbors."

Talia shook her head, but Reilly smiled gently.

"I don't want to convert you, Talia. We don't do much of that around here. Just think about it."

❄

When applause broke out at the end of *Bill*, Talia nearly dropped the chipped mug of chicken soup she'd been nursing in the back lot. She didn't, but the soup sloshed over the rim and her spoon went clattering to the dirty asphalt. She turned to find Jojo Moretz standing in the kitchen door.

Jojo clapped enthusiastically again. "Oh, Talia. I'm sorry about your lunch! Though I'd be lying if I said I was sorry for lurking while you finished. I could listen to you all day, and nobody sings songs from *Showboat* around here."

Talia flushed. "My mother had all those Broadway shows on records. I knew them all by heart before I even knew they were plays."

Memories of her mother were like cigar burns on her heart.

Jojo sat herself down next to Talia. "My first job when I left here for New York was as a rehearsal pianist for an off-broadway production company. I'd hear a great old song in an audition and end up scouring this little record shop on Thompson Street for the cast recording, and leaving with five more the old guy who ran it recommended." She fished a butterscotch from her pocket. "You want one?"

When Talia refused Jojo went on, the candy in her cheek. "I'm hosting book club this week. Tonight at my place. You should come."

Talia started to refuse, but Jojo was faster.

"Nobody reads the books. We just have snacks and wine and gossip. And there's a youth group social tonight at the church. My girlfriend runs it with Reilly. Eli will be welcome, and he's over there already."

If Talia's laugh was touched with bitterness, Jojo was kind enough to overlook it. "You've sewn me up, haven't you?"

Jojo inclined her head. Regally. "It's my gift. I am a ninja-level meddler."

"Please don't take this the wrong way," Talia said, bracing for Jojo to do exactly that, "but I'm not a joiner, and I'm not—we're not—religious."

Jojo leaned in close. "Half the folks who show up every Sunday would say the same. It's pretty laid back, the way we do things. Lots of people come for company and free coffee, or a chance to sit with their thoughts. Reilly's got enough faith for the whole town, but even he's... well... Still waters, I guess. His God had room for Jasmine and I long before most people. He's got more love in that crusty heart than he knows what to do with, but he's never settled down." She cackled. "Lord, I sound like such a *yenta*."

Hank's voice boomed from somewhere inside the diner. "Talia!"

Jojo stood. "Six tonight. 1280 Washington. Two blocks down on the left, above the storefront that sells all the teas and oils."

Talia couldn't think of a single argument. "Okay. Thanks."

Jojo waggled her fingers and vanished into the kitchen, her voice cutting through the diner noise as Talia followed. "Hank, you work that girl too hard. Is there coffee?"

Inside, there were two orders for mid-afternoon breakfast sandwiches and a to-go mac and cheese. Talia split two English muffins and broke a couple of eggs on the griddle, and tried to ignore the bubble of of nerves and curiosity in her belly.

Reilly was single.

Jojo wanted to be friends.

Eli hadn't complained at all about his time at the Grove Street Church, not since before the first day, and now he was being invited to youth group socials.

Reilly was single.

Talia flipped one pair of eggs to break the yolks and shimmied the second to keep them from sticking while the sunny yolks set. She caught herself humming *We Need A Little Christmas*, and smiled. Jojo would like that one, too.

Book club. She didn't go to book clubs.

Reilly was single.

✳

The Grove Street Church occupied a plot of land in a residential area a few blocks from the center of town. Not such a long walk from Jojo's apartment over the tea shop, but a cold one on a dark December night. The lights were on, glowing golden over the front doors, and Talia slipped into the vestibule. Reilly held court on the steps to the choir, a group of teens sprawled around him. There were a couple of guitars, a hand drum, and a harmonica, and in the middle of a motley crew of kids, her son. Talia's heart flipped over. Somewhere between moves, he'd developed a man's jawline and long limbs that spoke of more height to come.

He looked... content. In a way she hadn't seen in too long.

If only his father could see past what he believed his son should become to the young man he was.

If only Blaine could see life beyond his family.

If only.

And yet, her heart was still warm from boxed pinot grigio and Christmas cookies with Jojo's friends, who, after a few goggle-eyed moments, embraced her. Reilly chose that moment to look up from a spirited rendition of *Jingle Bells* that included some actual sleigh bells, and Talia grinned. Not only her heart, then. There was probably a commandment about not coveting thy neighborhood pastor, but the dimple in his left cheek was enough to bring a strong woman to her knees.

"Talia," he called across the hall. "Come in. We're just waiting for everyone's rides. You can pick up the harmony line."

And there it was, the wanting something from her.

"I'm sorry, Reverend." She made her way down the aisle; Eli scowled at her tone, and Talia's resolve faltered. "We have to get home. I'm sure Eli has homework."

Eli closed himself off. "I did it after school."

The ease she'd seen in Eli from across the room was gone, and an awkward silence fell over the youth group.

Reilly set down his instrument and addressed them. "Guys, can you head down to the basement and put the chairs away? And Haley?" Here he singled out one young woman. "Can you take the bells and drum downstairs and make sure the lights are turned out?"

When Eli didn't get up, Reilly gave him a look. "You too." Eli slouched off, leaving Talia standing there, keenly aware she'd ruined everything.

"I didn't mean—" she began, but Reilly cut her off.

"You are both welcome here. It has nothing to do with whether or not you sing in the choir, or what your faith is, or what's dogging you."

Talia felt all the fear and hurt—and bone deep weariness—rise. "Who said anything about my past?"

"No one but you. Just now," he said softly, and she knew he was right.

"You tricked me." Even as the words escaped her

mouth she knew how foolish she sounded.

"Talia." He said her name with a tenderness that shocked her. "Maybe it's what I do for a living, but I can see the hurt, the walls around you, from miles away."

Her reply came out as a whisper. "I didn't ask you to fix me."

When he closed the distance between them, coming to within arm's length, she wondering crazily if he was going to kiss her. "I don't want to fix what isn't broken. I just want to…"

He didn't finish the sentence. She couldn't look away.

Eli and Haley burst up from the church basement, laughing, his surly mood dissolved. The rest of the youth group thundered up behind them.

Reilly blinked at the pair of teens. "Lights out?"

The girl—Haley—laughed. "Yes, Pastor Hunt."

Talia watched the way her son looked at the girl. The very way she'd been looking at Reilly a moment ago.

"Eli, we should go."

Eli shrugged, but the girl only smiled. "See you at school, Eli."

❄

My mom doesn't like Christmas, the boy had said. *Or staying put.*

No one who sang Christmas songs like Talia Benson didn't like Christmas, but Reilly filed that bit of teenage insight away to worry over later. The hungry look on Eli Slattery's face when they'd trimmed the church giving tree for Sunday's service spoke volumes.

Reilly stopped at Snowflake Greens and Trees, the annual December pop-up tree lot in the market parking lot, and picked up a four-foot Fraser fir with a simple stand and a couple of strings of lights. There were boxes of red glass globes for sale, too, so he picked one of those up too. Eli was staying late at school to work on a project with Haley Jay and some of her friends, so Reilly didn't expect him for a volunteer shift. He figured he'd drop the festive supplies off at Talia's house with a note, before heading home to finish the Christmas Eve service from the comfort of his couch.

The slick Mercedes SUV in her driveway surprised him. Reilly pulled his beat up Ford in behind it and cut the engine. He was hoisting the tree out of the bed when the driver of the Mercedes pushed his way out of his ride. The dark, elegant suit could have paid Talia's rent for a couple of months; Reilly noted tasteful cufflinks and an expensive timepiece before the stranger smashed a fist into his jaw.

His head snapped back and stars bloomed behind his eyes, but he held it together. There was blood in his mouth, he spat it out. "What the hell?"

The stranger's eyes were flat and cold. "Stay the fuck away from my wife."

"Talia?"

Reilly knew he was provoking the flashy psychopath, but he figured they were already past pleasantries. When the suit pinned him the the cab of his truck by the windpipe, black fog narrowed his vision.

"My wife. *Natalia Slattery*, asshole."

In what remained of Reilly's consciousness, he recalled splashy headlines. The heir to a global shipping and real estate empire, a concert soprano, allegations of abuse... Reilly tried to suck in a breath, but the starry blackness was creeping inward. A car door slammed somewhere far away.

"Jesus, Blaine! Let him go!"

Oxygen flooded his lungs, and Reilly slumped back against the truck. Feeling returned to his face in the form of a throbbing jaw. Talia was running across the the frozen grass. She hit the stranger at a full run, pushing the man backwards towards the Mercedes. "He's a pastor, you crazy bastard. What is *wrong* with you?"

The man—Blaine—put his suit and tie to rights and cleared his throat. He sneered at Reilly. "Does he know you're not much an angel, babe?"

Talia's cheeks flushed scarlet, but she said nothing. Reilly pulled his phone from his pocket and tapped the emergency numbers.

Blaine looked at his watch. "Where's Elijah? I'm taking him home for Christmas."

"No, Blaine. You're not. He was quite clear the last time you tried that. You terrify him."

"Only because you poisoned his mind against me."

"You did that on your own." Talia squared her shoulders. "Leave us alone, Blaine. We don't want you."

Blaine's arm whipped up. Reilly heaved himself up to defend Talia, but Blaine only grabbed her arm and hauled her close. "I don't think you get it. I don't care. I want my family where they belong."

The officer that rolled up pulled his Interceptor onto the shoulder in front of Talia's house and stepped out of the SUV. Reilly recognized him from Hank's. "Is there a problem, ma'am? Are you okay? Reverend Hunt?"

Reilly watched Talia, who stared hard at Blaine.

Blaine released Talia and stepped back.

Her voice wavered slightly. "I think Mr. Slattery is leaving."

Blaine climbed into and backed the SUV around his truck and out of Talia's driveway. Reilly's head swam; he'd never been a brawler. Talia, it seemed, was made of sterner stuff. She came to him, touched his tender jaw with steady fingers.

"He hurt you."

Reilly felt that touch to his toes. "Has he hurt you?"

"Not my body, if that's what you mean." Her smile twisted at the corner. "It's a long, terrible story, but Reilly?"

Reilly held her gaze. "Yeah?"

"I'm not his wife."

His jaw ached like fury, but he was smiling some when he walked with her to speak with the officer who was watching Slattery's tail lights in the distance.

❄

Reilly took up more space in the kitchen than she'd expected. She'd made a compress for his jaw out of a package of frozen corn and a washcloth, and offered to make him dinner while they waited for Haley's mom to drive Eli home.

That he had thought to arrange that with Mrs. Jay was something Talia didn't like to dwell on. It was too easy to depend on that kind of thoughtfulness.

She set plates of scrambled eggs and sliced flank steak down and sat, hoping the food would prevent Reilly from asking the questions she was certain he must have. Butter padded out from Eli's bedroom and laid his traitorous head down in Reilly's lap.

"You are a woman of many talents," he said, chewing his meat carefully. "Who taught you to cook?"

"My mom," she said, salting her eggs. She inhaled deeply, deciding he'd earned some answers, and speared a mouthful of eggs. "She could make anything, except decent coffee. She died while I was in Las Vegas for a symphony gig."

"Natalia Benson." Reilly shook his head. "My folks have a recording of Christmas songs you did."

"That's the one." Recording that concert had been the highlight of her too-brief career. "The Las Vegas gig. *Oh, Night Divine: Natalia Benson and the Las Vegas Philharmonic Live at Christmas.* I found out my mother died after the concert, and got regrettably drunk at the hotel while my agent figured out a flight home. I met Blaine at the bar. He was handsome and charmingly concerned about me. I blacked out."

She looked up from her empty fork. Reilly's silverware rested on his place. His steady expression waited for her to go on, so she did.

"When I woke up, I was in Blaine's hotel room with a ring around my finger. He produced a marriage certificate. He told me I'd begged him, promised me I'd said yes, then made me feel awful when I didn't recall any of it. He offered to fly back with me, to meet my family. I was his wife now, after all. I was so numb that I let him sweep me around for months, and then I was pregnant. I let my career slip away. His family is…"

"Disgustingly, exploitively rich?" Reilly prompted.

"That's kind of you," Talia said. "I won't bore you with the Lifetime movie details of his illness and manipulations. I had Eli, and I woke up. In the hospital, doing paperwork for his birth certificate, it occurred to me that I never legally changed my name, only started using Slattery. I found out that our marriage was never real. It was essentially a year-long gaslighting by a very wealthy, very unwell man and his entire family."

"Talia…"

"No, it's… not okay, but it's something I've learned to look at objectively. His family used money and influence to keep him out of treatment and the press. When his mother found out our marriage was a sham, she offered to buy Eli from me, so I left."

"Buy him?" Reilly's voice was growly with shock.

"Five million if I'd walk away without my baby. Or nothing for either of us ever." Talia pushed her plate away. "So I checked us out of the hospital and disappeared. I was never very famous; it wasn't hard to disappear. I even like who I am now, but when Blaine gets away from his handlers he hunts me down, and the whole circus starts again."

Reilly stood, collected their uneaten suppers and took them to the counter, Butter watching his movements with canine optimism. Talia watched in a confused silence while he riffled through her cabinets and drawers until he'd found plastic wrap and put the plates in the fridge. He ran the hot water tap for a moment before digging into the remaining dishes, which he washed and set in the drying rack with surprising efficiency. When he was done, he pulled his chair up close to hers, and sat so they were eye to eye.

"You are incredible."

She laughed, but the earnestness in his eyes loosened a knot she'd had so long she'd forgotten it, and tears pooled in her eyes. "I'm a disaster."

He reached across the space between them to brush a stray tear from her cheek. Warmth spread from his fingertips, and she leaned into his palm.

"We're all disasters," he whispered, then touched his lips to hers.

She let her eyes drift closed, savoring the kiss.

When Reilly drew back, Talia opened her eyes to his dimpled smile. The dog wiggled between them.

"Please don't run away this time."

❄

Christmas Eve dawned sunny and frosty. Talia woke to the smell of coffee and the jingle of Butter's collar. Hank's was closed for three days, and for a week, there had been no noise from Blaine. She wasn't foolish enough to think he'd forgotten, but his family would go to great lengths to avoid revealing just how unstable their son was, including keeping him on a short leash. The whiff of scandal that followed her disappearance had been enough to allow her time and leverage to get away the first time.

She pulled her hoodie over the camisole and leggings she'd slept in and followed the wafting cloud toward the kitchen.

Eli was buttering toast. "Morning, Mom. Merry

Christmas."

The little tree Reilly had brought them sparkled from the living room. She sat in the same chair he'd sat in when he kissed her a few nights before; this time Butter watched his boy hoping for a bread-shaped Christmas miracle. "You made coffee?"

Eli pushed the hair from his face. "Mrs. Jay showed me how. I didn't get you a present, but I made you breakfast." He set slightly limp toast and watery coffee on the table in front of her.

It was the best breakfast she'd ever had.

She wrapped an arm around his skinny waist and pulled her son close. "I love you, kiddo. Thanks for this."

"Mom?"

"Yeah?"

"I know it's not your thing, but can we go to one of the services at the church? Haley says…"

Talia raised an eyebrow. "Haley says?"

Eli blushed. "She sings in the choir, and she says it's not like regular church on Christmas Eve. Mostly music and stuff."

"We can go. *If* you watch Christmas movies with me all day, and we get Chinese for dinner."

The awkward eye-roll she got was worth it when he grinned.

The Grove Street Church was packed. The front doors were wreathed with balsam and bittersweet, rainbow flags welcomed congregants. Candles burned on the altar, and the choir was singing low in welcome, the *Coventry Carol*. Eli nudged her for humming along.

They took their places in a pew near the back of the hall. Talia's breath caught when Reilly stepped up to address his congregation; she glanced around, half-wondering if lightning might actually strike. He preached no differently than he lived: patiently and without fuss. He'd forgone celebratory robes; the only mark of his leadership was a clerical collar instead of a tie, and and a crimson stole over a conservative dark gray suit.

After a few brief words of welcome, the choir began *The First Noel*. She hadn't meant to sing at all, but her resolve vanished before the first line finished. At the chorus, when her voice soared over the gathering, there was a moment of astonished quiet from the congregation as people's voices faded to search for the source of hers, but just a moment. Reilly only smiled, Jojo turned with a wink from the choir, and every voice was lifted along with hers.

It was, as Haley told Eli, mostly music and stuff. Reilly told the Christmas story with humor and grace. He thanked the community for the toys and clothes gifted to the needy and called the younger members of the congregation up to sing with his guitar as accompaniment. Eli made no move to join them, until another boy from the youth group cuffed his shoulder on his way by. Talia couldn't help noticing Haley Jay smiling from the choir when Eli trailed the others to the steps.

When Reilly wished them all peace and joy for the new year and hoped they would find light in the dark season, she felt his gaze fall on her, and the heat that kindled along her skin had little to do with the candlelight or the closeness of bodies.

✳

After the service, Eli melted into the crowd to seek out his youth group cohort. Talia loitered near the vestibule, watching folks catching up and wishing one another merry Christmas.

Hank and his wife Gayle stopped to say hello, and another of the diner regulars tipped his hat before joining some friends.

She was so absorbed in her people watching, she didn't notice Jojo until the other woman sidled up next to her.

"Talia!" Jojo hugged her fiercely. Talia froze for a moment before the reality of Jojo's easy affection hit her. "Merry Christmas! Please, please, please sing with us?" She gestured to two other choristers standing nearby who smiled and nodded, then whispered, "I won't even tell them who you are."

Reilly was making his way along the center aisle, shaking hands and embracing his people. She could see it in his entire body, how much he loved them.

Jojo caught the direction of her gaze. "I hope it's okay that he told me what happened. It shook him up."

The warmth flickered, and an icicle formed in the pit of her stomach. There was only so much of her circus anyone could take. Even her son would tire of it, of her, someday. She sought out Eli among the teens huddled in one corner of the hall, and forced the corners of her lips back up. "Of course. Don't worry about it."

Jojo's brow wrinkled. "I'll worry if I like. You're ours now, you know. We don't take lightly to that kind of nonsense." She waved at Reilly over the tops of nearby heads, then gave Talia a significant look. "He doesn't, either."

Reilly approached her, hands in his pockets. There was a sparkle in his eyes that was just for her, and the icicle melted away. "Merry Christmas, Talia. I'm glad to see you here."

His closeness was intoxicating. "Merry Christmas, Reverend."

She wanted to fold herself into the curve of his shoulder, to rest her cheek in the hollow there.

Jojo leaned over and hugged him. "Merry Christmas, Doc."

A petite woman with long hair in a frazzled bun took Talia by the arm. "Talia? I'm Helena Jay, Haley's mom. I just wanted to say, Eli is great. Haley's taken him under her wing. I'm not sure whether to congratulate you or warn you. Honestly, she's a force. Anyway, merry Christmas."

Helena turned to Jojo and Reilly, but Talia sought out her son. He was part of this place already.

"... I'm going to get her to sing with us, Laney. Next Christmas she and Nancy are going to bring the house down."

Jojo was talking about her. Talia dropped back into the conversation before Reilly's Girl Friday could get her in trouble. Jojo and Helena had their heads together, but Reilly's expression was the one that stilled her. His smile was easy, but hope blazed in those kind eyes.

She was part of this place already.

Talia cleared her throat. "Is there music for Easter?"

Jojo whooped a hallelujah, and Reilly took her hand in his as the church bells rang in Christmas Day.

ABOUT THE AUTHORS

Angela Amman

Angela Amman is a short story and essay writer. Collecting her family's stories is a gift-in- progress for her daughter and son, and she blogs at Playing with Words, capturing the craziness and beauty that weave together to create something extraordinary. As a part of Listen To Your Mother Metro Detroit, Angela is thrilled to bring others' stories to the stage and to celebrate the magic of words, storytelling, and the courage to share that magic with an audience. She is a managing editor at Bannering Books, a small publishing imprint, and when she should be sleeping, she works on her novel. Her writing has been featured on Mamalode, BlogHer, Club Mid, and SheKnows. Her personal essays and short stories have appeared in her collection, *Nothing Goes Away*, and various fiction and non-fiction anthologies.

Mandy Dawson

Mandy Dawson, author and Baroness, lives with her two young children in a tiny cottage surrounded by roses where chickens eat her garden and Clark the Cat hisses at any attempt at petting. She's been writing since the fourth grade when she created a novel set in the fictional Western town of Calamine named for the lotion because it sounded exotic. Mandy has written for *Momtastic*, *BlogHer*, *Mamapedia*, *VProud*, and has appeared on HuffPost Live.

Cameron D. Garriepy

An Aries, a self-described shenaniganist, and an

unabashed romantic, Cameron writes romantic fiction and genre-crossing short stories from the metro-Boston area, where she lives with her husband, son, and a poorly behaved pug.

In the eighth grade, she wrote her first romance novel on an antique typewriter, using a stack of pink paper. Detours between that draft and publishing her first novel included a BA in Music from Middlebury College, a professional culinary education, and twelve years in the child-wrangling industry.

Cameron's adventures in flash fiction can be found on her blog. Formerly, she was an editor at Write on Edge, and she is the founder of and senior editor at Bannerwing Books.

An excerpt from
SWEET PEASE
by Cameron D. Garriepy

"I'm going to make one hell of a maid of honor."

Kate Pease laughed off the wobble in her voice and blinked back a threatening tear. She smoothed the fuchsia silk shantung over her hips and stomach, twisting to check out her own rear view in the three-way mirror.

Her best friend, Nan Grady, stood on a dressmaker's pedestal while an attendant laced up the wedding gown she was trying on. Nan was radiant; the creamy silk only accentuated her glow.

Kate blinked back tears. It wasn't every day your best friend found the dress she was going to get married in. "That's the one, you know."

Nan blushed happily. "I think so, too."

"There's no thinking about it. It's the one."

The two women regarded each other. Below the second story window, Boston's Newbury Street bustled despite the January cold. Nan's brilliant smile wavered;

Kate rushed over and swiped gently at the yet-to-fall wetness in her friend's eyes.

"No crying. We are far too fabulous today for streaky mascara."

Lady Gaga suggested a bad romance from Kate's purse. When Nan snickered, Kate shot her friend a withering look.

She retrieved her phone from the bag and took the call with a grin. "Hello, brother dear."

"Did Nan pick a dress?"

"Yes, she found her dress." Kate winked at Nan, who was posing for the shop attendant's measuring tape.

"Did you leave anything for the other shoppers?"

Her brother Jack might taunt her about her shopping habit, but his own was just as bad… if not worse.

"You're mean."

"Can I make it up to you with an extravagant lunch?"

"You can."

"I have to go; client on the other line."

He gave her a restaurant name and a time, and Kate ended the call.

Nan looked over her shoulder while the attendant created a potential bustle in the skirt. "Lunch?"

"At that sushi place near Jack's office. And he's picking up the tab."

Kate watched as Nan took a moment to drink in her own reflection. The dress was a simple A-line; the corsetry emphasized Nan's lean waist and gentle curves. The skirt clung to her hips just a little before falling like water to her feet.

"Oh, Nan," Kate breathed, "you're gorgeous."

Thornton was in for the wedding of the decade. The Fullers, the Peases—who considered Nan one of their own already—and nearly half the county would gather to celebrate Nan and Joss Fuller's marriage at the Damselfly in June.

That they would all eat cake by Kate Pease, well that

didn't hurt either. Especially given her business plans.

Placing the dress order was swift and expensive. Her thrifty friend was pale with sticker shock. Kate squeezed Nan's hand in solidarity.

Kate and Nan gathered coats and scarves and gloves, bundling up against the bluster of a Boston winter. Just as they struck out for the T station at Arlington Street, Nan's phone rang in her pocket.

"Hello, Anna?" Nan motioned for Kate to stop. "He just walked in? Well, we have room. Go ahead and check him in."

While Nan walked her friend and inn-sitter through the registration software, Kate's gaze lingered on a camel hair wool skirt in the window of a nearby boutique, and she slipped inside.

Kate picked up a few additional items on her way to the fitting room. Nan followed her inside. Her half of the conversation was clear across the tiny space.

"I'm as surprised as you are." Nan's smile was wide and gleeful. "I can't imagine why, though. The college must have offered him an apartment."

Kate waved to Nan, motioning at the fitting room door while Nan's eyes widened at whatever Anna was saying.

"He's what?" Nan laughed aloud. "I have to go. Kate and I are meeting Jack for lunch before we drive home. I'll be home in plenty of time for you to tuck Chloe in."

Nan waved to Kate from across the sales floor, pointed at her watchless wrist.

"Bye, Anna. Thanks for calling. Give Chloe a snuggle for me."

Kate whipped through her choices, but nothing was just right. She hung everything on the rack outside the fitting room and sought Nan out among the scarves near the register. She tucked her arm in Nan's and swept them out the door and down the street.

"What did Anna want?"

Nan squinted into the glittering winter sun. "I have a new guest. A surprise. Anna says he, and I quote, 'looks like Mr. Rochester.'"

"Oh, really?" Visions of Timothy Dalton's smoldering gaze danced in her head. She silently thanked her mother for making her watch old BBC dramas when she was home sick in high school. "I always did think Rochester was kind of dreamy."

Nan snorted. "Don't."

Kate grinned, wondering if the newcomer was her kind of dreamy.

And if he was single.

~~~

Ewan's temporary office on the fourth floor of Keller Hall was quiet and devoid of personal effects. He'd brought little with him on this first visit, just a small, framed lithograph of the Chrysler building and a photograph of his parents standing on the stoop of the Brooklyn Heights apartment building where he had grown up, both of which fit in his laptop bag.

Reed Sharpe's galley taunted him from his desk like a malevolent paperweight. He turned instead to the view over County Road, just in time to watch a sleek sports car roar over the ridge and downshift with a throaty purr as it whipped down the hill that bisected the campus.

He smiled at the blur of the car hugging the curve below the science building. Maybe things didn't move so slowly in the country after all.

Thornton College, nestled in two hundred years of tradition and rustic Vermont hillside, was breathtaking, but it was neither the ivy-draped white granite buildings around the quad nor the charming village straddling the river that thrilled him about this position.

It was a chance to research a tenuous connection between his family and Thornton's best-kept ghost story.

There was a novel in it; he just had to find the lost threads of the tale.

A knock at the door pulled Ewan from his thoughts. The intrusion didn't bother him so much as surprise him. He pushed aside the Sharpe novel and took off his reading glasses.

"Come in."

"Excuse me, Professor Lovatt?" A young man in Elvis Costello frames and a Navy surplus pea coat shuffled into the room.

"Mmhm?"

"I'm Ryan Chandler. I write for *The Rose and Talon*. I'd love to do a piece on you for our next issue."

"The *Rose and Talon*?"

"Online daily broadsheet. Thornton, the rose. Falcon, the talon. We started it as a side project for our freshman Shakespeare seminar."

"Clever. All right, Ryan. Have a seat." He gestured to the empty academic chair across the room. The boy pulled the chair up to the opposite side of Ewan's desk and pulled out his smartphone. He unwound a preposterously long, striped scarf from his neck and draped it over the chair, revealing a hipster band T-shirt whose logo Ewan actually recognized.

"Do you mind if I record this?" Ryan gestured to the phone.

"Nope."

Pulling a composition notebook and a gel pen from the front pocket of his bag, the boy touched the screen of his phone and spoke.

"Interview with Professor Ewan Lovatt. Office 402, Keller Hall, Thornton College, January twenty-eight." He looked up at Ewan. "Well, Professor, how are you finding Thornton?"

"I've only just arrived. I checked into the Damselfly Inn yesterday."

"And how are you enjoying it?"

"Charming."

"Charming?" The boy echoed. "Your characters, especially Dearest in *Moriarty's Daughter*, often use one word replies to deflect attention from their private agendas. Would you say this is something you do as well?"

His interviewer had at least read the right reviews of his work. "I suppose all authors draw on themselves a little."

"That's a very diplomatic answer."

Ewan chuckled. "My room is very comfortable. Ms. Grady is a generous hostess. My breakfast scone was a little dry. Probably the last one of the morning."

He watched the young journalist notice the Reed Sharpe novel and switch tacks. "The critics loved your last two novels, but I've read that *Moriarty's Daughter* was passed over by a major Hollywood studio while Reed Sharpe's Hawk Johnson books are being optioned for a multi-film series. Authors like him are more of a hit with bestseller lists and Hollywood executives. Does that ever factor into your writing style?"

"Not particularly." He didn't want to talk about Reed Sharpe.

Ryan was quick to take that in. "You self-published your first few books, the Alasdair Sledge novellas, which you've continued to put out between your traditionally backed literary fiction. There are a lot of people who wonder why a man, whose historical female leads are so treasured, also writes a steampunk mystery series with no women at all."

Ewan went for levity. "Alasdair just hasn't found the right woman yet."

"Is that autobiographical?"

Ryan Chandler wasn't half bad at interviewing. Ewan reached for his glasses, though he didn't need them. "Just a coincidence."

"You're offering an intro to speculative fiction, a

junior seminar in novella structure, and an independent project opportunity in literary fiction. Those are some very interesting course options. Are these courses you've taught before?"

"They are. I'm also co-instructing a course in publishing industry legal issues with Will Dancy."

Ryan consulted his notebook. "You've taught at NYU, Emory, and UVA over the last few years. That's an impressive spread. What drew you to Thornton?"

The Damselfly Inn. Ewan pushed aside the true answer and gave his interviewer the quote he needed for the piece. "I'd heard the students here were some of the best minds I could learn from."

Ryan laughed out loud. "Well-played, Professor. I won't take any more of your time. I appreciate you talking with me."

"Not a problem," Ewan said. "I'll keep an eye out for that broadsheet of yours."

"The profile will be online around midnight. I'll be sure to send you a link."

"You do that."

"Good day, Professor."

Ryan stood, made a production of buttoning the six buttons on his coat and winding his scarf just-so, shouldered his expensive messenger bag, and hunched his way out into the corridor. Ewan leaned back in his chair and kicked his boots onto his desk. The Reed Sharpe novel hit the floor with a solid thump. At nearly five hundred pages, the damn thing would make an excellent weapon. He let it lie where it had fallen and watched students trickling out of the granite and ivy buildings which ringed the quad. Winter term was finishing up; the campus was preparing for a short break and a new semester.

His student interviewer had come closer to the heart of the matter than he could have known. Thornton held the key to the next stage of his career.

Chasing Strollers, an excerpt from
GARDEN BOULEVARD
coming 2018 from Angela Amman

Nora still brought the stroller when they walked, even
though Josie would only sit in it for seconds at a time. It
had bothered her at first, how slow their daily outings
went without Josie contained. Nora's legs didn't
remember how to move at a toddler's pace, and she'd feel
impatience and embarrassment collide until tears sprang
into her eyes. Matt laughed them away.

"Nora, love, what did you think it would mean to
raise her here? That she'd pick up the ability to speed
walk before she even learned how to write her name?"

"I hate feeling like we're in the way," Nora countered.

"You're always in someone's way here," he said. "It's
part of the city's inexplicable charm, the way you annoy
the people around you just by existing."

She laughed, the way she always did when Matt
buffered her from the loneliness of spending all her time
with a little person who mostly talked about stuffed
animals and tea parties. His generously-poured mimosas
helped, too, but Nora hadn't stopped wishing Josie would
walk more quickly until the day she started running,

threading through the crowd like a torpedo.

Nora abandoned the stroller to chase her daughter, both of them a little shocked when she finally caught Josie and promptly burst into tears. Throngs of people had pushed the stroller to the side, one wheel caught in a sidewalk crack, spinning helplessly. Josie rode home that day, the clatter of the wheels against the concrete lulling her to sleep in a way it hadn't in almost a year, and Nora resigned herself to living in a perpetual state of legs moving too quickly or too slowly.

One day she noticed she didn't feel embarrassed anymore. Josie still stopped just as frequently to look at twinkling chunks of broken glass or the way weeds poked through the sidewalk, but Nora simply planted her feet on both sides of her child, letting walkers stream around her. They grumbled, but Nora no longer heard the words because she concentrated on Josie's burgeoning vocabulary. But she still toted along the stroller, just in case.

"Mama, we go get a cookie today?" Josie asked hopefully, staring out the window one afternoon after a particularly productive nap.

"No, sweets. Remember we talked about not eating giant cookies every day? Besides, I'm fairly sure a certain little girl didn't eat any of her carrots or her broccoli at lunch."

Josie's eyes widened as her nose crinkled. A huge sigh escaped her lungs, and Nora tried not to laugh as Josie pushed her hair back from her face with both palms. She knew the gesture intimately, her own hands pushing her own hair back from her face in exactly the same way.

"Mama. Boppy never eats her carrots, and she can have cookies seven times a day," Josie said.

Boppy didn't protest, the worn elephant half-stuffed under Josie's pillow.

"Maybe Boppy would like to walk over to the

playground, even without a cookie," Nora suggested. Their daily walks were as much a part of their routine as tapas-style meals and the nap Josie recently started protesting. Even in rain and snow they tramped around for a few blocks, though on the snowiest days Nora would leave the stroller home. They never went far enough to risk getting stuck in the snow.

"Sure, Mama," Josie agreed.

She plucked Boppy from the pillow and snuggled him into her face before nuzzling Nora's face with the over-loved fur. Nausea swept through Nora's body, sweat beading on her forehead. Her stomach had protested almost everything she touched the last few days, and apparently a utilitarian lunch of chicken salad and Nora's leftover veggies wasn't faring well. She scrambled to the bathroom near Nora's nursery, vowing to toss Boppy in the washer with the next load of clothes so he'd be fresh and ready for bedtime snuggles.

"What're you doing?" Josie demanded, face scrunched in a mix of uncertainty, worry, and distaste.

"Mama's not feeling well," Nora said. She cringed at the way she addressed herself in the third person. She hadn't spoken like that to Josie in what seemed like an eternity, those early years of constant vocabulary-building fading away into hazy memories.

"You want to hold Boppy?" Josie held out the elephant, though she looked more than relieved when Nora shook her head. "Missuz Lodi would get you a tube."

Nora felt laughter bubbling behind her ribs, competing with her roiling stomach for attention. "Mrs. Lodi, indeed, would likely have an essential oil roller for Ma—for me. I'm okay now, sweets. Let's get to the park and swing."

~~~

Two hours later, Nora leaned against the back of the park bench, careful not to let the splintery wood poke too closely to her skin. She felt like leaving but wondered if her legs would get her safely back to their apartment. Josie continued her loop around the play structure, a glaze of little girl sweat and dirt plastering curls to her temples. Nora let her neck rest against the back of the bench. If only she could close her eyes for just a moment. All of her conviction that they lived in a safe neighborhood wouldn't allow her to fall prey to the song of sunshine and sleepiness.

"Mama!" Josie's voice cut through the fog of exhaustion.

"Yes, Jojo?"

"I think I want a snack now," Josie said, eyes fixed on the pretzel vendor near the entrance to the park.

She had said no to the cookie idea, but even Nora didn't think she could resist the lure of salt and warm bread mere footsteps away. Josie lofted herself onto the bench beside her mother as Nora dug in her small messenger bag for cash. Her eyes snagged on a mother near the swings, digging through a behemoth of a tote. Nora remembered those days, when she had carried around a bag spilling diapers and sippy cups. A thought niggled in her skull, disquieting her, but she turned back to her daughter with a crumpled ten-dollar bill in her hand.

"Do you think you might share your giant pretzel with me?" Nora asked.

Josie nodded and planted a kiss on Nora's nose. "Thanks, Mama!"

Nora inhaled Josie's scent: earth, warmth, and peach-scented shampoo Josie chose based on how much she liked the bottle. The stroller rolled in front of her with one hand, while she tucked Josie's fingers into the palm of her other. Josie's confident voice negotiated the exchange of food for money, but Nora held the pretzel in her own hand, weaving the stroller toward the other side of the cart. Instinctively, she grabbed the mustard, prepared to smear a bit onto her half of the warm pretzel, but the wafting scent turned her stomach again. Almost as if on cue, a baby down the block began to cry, and bits and pieces of the last six weeks slid into place like tumblers clicking in a lock.

She barely remembered their walk home, except for the freedom she felt walking with her child's hand in hers and the stroller in the other, her untouched pretzel nestled in napkins on the seat of the stroller.

~~~

A lifetime later, Matt walked through the door. He closed it quietly, but even the subtle noise startled her into consciousness from where she'd fallen asleep on the couch. She dodged his tie as he leaned over to kiss her hello, the cigarettes he pretended not to smoke reminding her of a time when they'd wander to the sidewalk outside of bars and talk until they forgot to go back inside.

"Did you and Jojo try that new yoga class today?"

"No, that's not until next week. Just the park today." Her voice didn't relay the panic circling her brain. "Josie just had leftovers for dinner. Do you want to call for something?"

He sank next to her on the small sofa, and she slid her finger under the loosened tie, reading his day by the deepness of the furrows in his brow, and watching his eyes trail to the edge of the cluttered ottoman.

"Why's the baby monitor out here?" They hadn't needed it once they discovered Josie wouldn't spontaneously combust if they didn't watch each moment of her nap.

She had almost forgotten taking Josie with her to ransack their small storage area after dinner.

"It doesn't work anymore," she started.

He nodded, his patience calming her worry, but only slightly.

"I'm pregnant," she blurted.

He blinked, then a smile cracked open his face.

"I didn't even realize it was a possibility right now," he said. His arms circled her, lips pressed against her forehead. She could feel the steady thud of his heart and tried to concentrate on its rhythm. Everything in her own body felt foreign and off-kilter.

"I'm pregnant, and our baby monitor doesn't even work," she said.

Laughter rumbled in his chest. "So we'll get a new monitor," he started, but his voice changed when he saw the brightness of tears in her eyes. "Oh, hey, Nor. This is a good thing, isn't it?"

"Yes?" She couldn't make her answer anything other than a question.

"I know we haven't talked about it in a while, but I always thought..."

"No. I know. I mean, we never planned on having Josie be our only child. I'm just scared shitless I won't be able to make this work, you know?"

Confusion battled with excitement in his face, and part of her hated she hadn't come to terms with the pregnancy before tossing it into the space between them. But she'd never hidden anything from him, especially not something that affected both of them irrevocably.

"What do you mean, love? You're a killer mom."

"I'm her mom, though, and I barely have that figured out. How am I supposed to push her stroller and hold a baby and carry a damn diaper bag again?"

He sighed, just enough for her to hear and she backpedaled a little. "I'm not suggesting we leave the city. I know you don't want to do that, and I don't even want to do that anymore, but...."

"But you're kind of suggesting it?" The probing

question was gentler than she expected, a contrast to the heated arguments they had about it for months after Josie started crawling, shrinking their apartment into minuscule proportions.

His chest had always been the most comfortable place to rest, and she couldn't bring herself to look into his eyes quite yet.

"I don't know," she admitted.

"Listen, love, we don't have to decide anything tonight," he said. She could hear the smoothness of his voice, the one she always imagined he used during his most explosive client meetings, but she was too exhausted to worry she was being placated.

"Let's get tacos," she said. "I can't think of anything that sounds good to eat except a vat of guacamole."

He grinned, smoothing back her hair.

"We're having another baby," he said. She let the seed of his excitement bury itself in her chest and take bloom, just a smidge. She kept her eyes off the hallway, where the doors would remind her of Josie's small room and the even smaller third bedroom that was scarcely more than a closet.

~~~

Matt was gone by the time she woke the next morning, her alarm quietly chiming her to life so she could make coffee before her daughter's chatter overwhelmed her day. He left a text for her from the train, a few words reminding her of how thrilled he was about their news.

Her single brewer worked its magic quickly, and she lazily wondered if the caffeine recommendations for pregnant women had changed since her last pregnancy. Instead of a quick internet search that might make her feel guilty, she liberally poured flavored creamer and sipped in ignorant bliss for at least one more day. A moment later, she heard tiny feet hit the ground running, and she felt claustrophobia threaten as she imagined a crib geometrically wedged into the sparse space in which they lived.

"Morning, Jojo," she said, peppering her daughter's unruly curls with kisses. "Let's go get an egg sandwich from the deli."

Josie looked delighted with the unexpected treat, and they both dressed quickly. Nora imagined she felt a swelling under the waistband of her favorite jeans already, but she shook her head at herself. Right now the only thing she wanted to do was get out of the apartment and get a little bit of air.

On the sidewalk, she immediately worried she'd made a mistake. The bustle of commuters still clogged the streets, and she felt Josie's fingers pulling her forward through the ocean of people. Instead of fresh air, she felt assaulted by expensive perfume and gourmet coffee steaming from familiar white cups that had once been ubiquitously cardboard.

Only steps from the crosswalk, Josie stopped abruptly. Almost on top of her daughter, Nora looked down. Josie had assumed one of her favorite positions, crouched over the sidewalk, hands splayed on her knees as she keenly observed a cluster of rose petals on the ground. Even Nora felt drawn to them, red satin ovals tumbled onto the concrete in small clusters. Before she could stop Josie, the little girl scooped a bunch of them between her hands and stood, pressing them toward Nora.

"Look Mama! I found you some flowers," she said.

Nora let herself inhale their perfume.

Josie clapped her hands in excitement, and the petals drifted back to the ground.

"I always find such beautiful things when we walk." Josie's sigh of contentment sounded exactly like Matt, and Nora knew, somehow, their baby would fit into their city life just perfectly.

An excerpt from
ELEMENTAL ESCAPE
coming 2018 from Mandy Dawson

When Weston Remmings VII was five years old, he
carelessly told his parents he wanted to be a firefighter
when he grew up. His mother's face paled while his
father's normally placid expression turned red with rage.
The slap across Weston's face stung less than the months
of silent disapproval.

"You mustn't be angry with him," his mother had
counseled in her softly accented voice. "He doesn't want
you to dream. It's far too dangerous." She had kissed his
tear stained cheeks while he wiggled into her warm
lavender embrace.

When Weston was nine years old, he knew better
than to voice his dream of being an artist. By that point,
he knew he was unlike the children he saw in books and
on television. He watched their neon clad bodies slouch
onto couches from his position in a hard backed chair.
Unlike the acid washed jeans and spiked hair on the
screen, he wore a daily uniform of black slacks, a crisp
white shirt, and dark hair parted precisely three inches
above his left ear. His tie was always neatly knotted, it's

color determined by Her mood.

He never called her by name — even in the secret corners of his mind. She was always ma'am, her, she. In his family's isolated world, there was only one She. The others who lived in the estate avoided his eyes when passing, quickening their pace to avoid him.

"They know," his mother had whispered into his hair. "They know you are special and chosen."

Even as a boy of nine, he understood the lie. The others avoided him because they knew she could hear his every thought, see his every memory and none of them wanted to bring attention to themselves, to draw Her eye was dangerous.

When Weston was ten years old, he began his training, a silent shadow to his father. He kept all thoughts of rebellion and escape carefully tucked into a corner of his mind he dared not venture while looking into a future he could predict with absolute certainty.

The first time She saw him, Weston was twenty years old.

"Remmings," she said in her cool voice, "fetch Marcus."

Weston's father hastened to do his mistress's bidding. She held up one slim finger. He froze mid-step. Her voice sharpened. "Are you deaf? Fetch Marcus."

Weston looked into her cruel golden eyes and knew his training was over. "Yes, ma'am." Weston bowed crisply from the waist and, without a glance at his father, left the room.

That night Weston climbed the stairs to his family's quarters and opened a door to an empty apartment, every trace of his parents gone as if they'd never existed.

Perhaps, he thought as he stared blankly into the mirror above the bathroom sink, they never had.

He pulled the razor through the white foam coating his face, erasing any trace of shadow. Setting the razor precisely where his father had always placed his, he looked into his father's blue eyes. His bleak existence stretched ahead like a night devoid of stars and moon.

He was Remmings. There was nothing else for him.

~~~

All legs and long blond hair, she looked at him through eyes of ice blue. Even in captivity those eyes snapped with fury and power. He drank in the sight of her. Even with her hair hanging limp and knotted around a bruised face, the purple stark against pale skin, she was still the most beautiful woman he'd ever seen.

He rolled the cart through the doors. She watched him from beneath her lashes. He snapped a table cloth over the plain plastic folding table with an efficiency born of experience. It fell perfectly, the edges needing little straightening. As he bent to recover the single place setting sitting neatly in the cart, he stole a glance at her.

Her eyes watched every movement and bore into him as if she could see what was left of his soul. Blood trickled from her nose, dripping unheeded to her dirt stained pants.

"It's not going to work, you know," a cool voice said from behind him. He snapped to attention as She walked into the cell. Her heels clattered across bare stone until She stood looking down on the woman at her feet.

"Where's Douglas, Avani?" Her voice sent an unfamiliar heat down Remmings spine. He trained his eyes on the stone wall, keeping his mind carefully blank and squirreling away the sensation of honey pooling in his stomach to examine away from Her all-knowing eyes.

His Lady's lips twisted into a snarl. He didn't flinch as the ground began to shake beneath them. "Dead."

He risked a look at the woman, surprised to see the tears pool in her eyes. Why would she cry for the man who had betrayed her? She blinked furiously, keeping the telling moisture from falling down her cheeks. "I can't imagine he went without a fight." The steel in her voice belied the warmth of tears.

Intelligence sharpened her gaze. "Where's Marcus? He likes looking at my legs."

"Remmings!" He took a step forward. "The tea is not going to pour itself." He sprang into action, setting a floral china cup on its saucer. He lifted the teapot, pouring it in a steady stream even as the woman's screams rent the air. He added milk, two sugars, and stirred, setting the spoon in an empty dish. He shifted his weight as a sailor might in the midst of a storm while the ground shook. He placed a small plate next to the cup and saucer, straightening it imperceptibly until Her favorite cake was featured in the midnight position. Swiping a thin metal blade across the white linen, he removed any traces of crumbs or sugar that may have evaded his careful eye.

The small room was silent but for the gasps coming from the woman huddled against the wall. He stepped back until he disappeared into the shadows, invisible to everyone but Her.

The woman lay on her side, blood mixing with tears. His Lady straightened Her hair, tucking a strand into the knot at the back of Her head. "Douglas is dead. My son," she spat the word, "might as well be." She bent and pushed the golden hair from a face covered in scrapes and scratches. "Stop thinking of escape. No one knows where you are or that you're still alive."

"Erik will come for me."

The crack of Her hand across the woman's face was an insult for one as powerful as the two women in the room. "Get that thought out of your head, dear." She laughed. "He knows where you are. He's abandoned you. You will talk or rot. Better yet," Her voice took on a tone of such tenderness, Remmings almost didn't recognize it, "keep thinking, Candace. Open your mind and it will all be over."

The woman closed her eyes and turned her head away.

"Very well." His Lady walked to the table and picked up her cup of tea with a hand smeared with blood. She took a sip and smiled the special smile She had when pleased with him. "Perfection, Remmings." Taking her tea and a small cake, she walked out the door, dismissing him.

Remmings stacked the dishes onto the shelf beneath the cart, lifting the cloth from the table and folding it into a precise square. He tucked it in its drawer and folded the table, snapping the legs closed. As he loaded the table, he looked at the woman huddled in a dirty heap on the floor. Her shoulders shook beneath the thin silk covering them.

Candace. He tested the name in his head before turning off the light and closing the door behind him. He turned the heavy key in its lock and walked down the corridor, his mind on the dinner menu, ignoring the sick feeling twisting his stomach at the memory of her screams.

~~~

Candace lifted her head as the light turned off, rolling as best she could into a more comfortable position. Douglas was dead. The damned idiot. Unrelenting darkness pressed upon her, bruising her more than Avani ever could. She leaned a cheek against the stone floor, straw rough against her cheek. Three days ago she'd been sitting neck deep in a bubble bath, a glass of wine on the stool next to the tub. She'd been fretting over the knowledge her world was about to explode.

She'd never doubted her safety.

Erik, she knew, would never let anything happen to her. As if she needed protection. She snorted, the sound turning into a laugh. If it tinged on hysterical, she could be forgiven.

She had never felt so utterly and completely alone.

"Think," she whispered into the darkness.

Her brain, usually her best feature, refused to move beyond a sluggish pace. She was tired, thirsty, hungry. She moved her head, wincing at the pain radiating from her temples. She breathed deeply, concentrating on channeling Air, hoping for some sort of movement to offer hope. She focused inward, letting her mind and body open. The pain was instant and intense. Fighting through it, she kept going, reaching for the thin wisp just beyond her reach.

A little more. Just a little more.

The pain increased until her ears began to ring and her hold to consciousness threatened snap.

She let go and fell back against the floor, gasping.

It was the collar. The stupid, ridiculous collar. She could feel it, pressed against her throat, constricting with each ragged breath.

Douglas, the damned idiot.

She let herself melt into the floor, the pain in her shoulders nothing compared to the pain in her head and heart. How could he have betrayed Erik? When had his loyalty shifted? Or had he always been in Avani's pocket?

How could he have betrayed her?

She'd known for decades how he felt about her. He hadn't exactly been subtle. She pictured the bear of a man, the irreverent grin that always danced in his eyes. If she was honest with herself, she had always thought at some point, perhaps after the danger had passed, they'd explore the spark that arced between them like electricity.

How had the damned idiot gotten into this mess?

She couldn't believe he'd always been a spy. He didn't have the guile. She thought back, retracing their steps.

She hadn't wanted to leave Erik, hadn't trusted the cold warrior he'd helped to resurrect. To be honest, she hadn't trusted Erik to get himself out of this mess alive.

She laughed bitterly, the sound startling in the silence. How the tables had turned. She didn't quite trust herself to get out of this mess alive. The alternative, while not ideal, was likely the best option.

She knew too much. Far too much. There were too many secrets filed away in her brain, far too many lives in her hands. What could Douglas have been thinking?

He'd come to her office, his bulk filling the doorway. She'd known instantly why he was there and hated him for it. She'd blamed him for holding her to a promise to Erik to leave at the first sign of trouble. She'd snapped at him, taking that frustration out on someone who seemed able to handle it.

She'd followed him out of the office building, to the car parked illegally in a red zone. It had irritated her, his disregard for the law. He'd held her door, his age showing in the chivalry he never seemed to be able to let go in this more modern era. He'd tried to talk to her. What had he said?

It seemed vitally important she remember the conversation. It was the last they'd had, the last time he'd spoken to her before leaving her with their enemy.

She closed her eyes and searched her foggy brain through the pain.

Flashes of light reflecting off the passing office buildings. She'd given him the silent treatment while he'd been almost cheerful, telling her about the cabin Erik had kept secret from even her. What had she finally said?

"You're okay leaving your friend just before battle?" She winced at the memory of the words, spoken in anger to a man who wouldn't live out the day.

"I know some things are too precious to risk." He'd been talking about her. Not her powers. Not her secret.

119

Her.

He'd turned from the road for a moment, his eyes sincere. "You're worth any risk, lass. Erik knows it. I know it."

She'd felt guilty for taking her anger out on him. Had she smiled? Offered an apology? The memories were too foggy, too far gone. Somehow, between that moment and the next, she'd been upside down, pinned to the car by nothing but her seatbelt. Douglas had been yelling, pulling at the straps holding her prisoner as smoked filled her lungs. She'd fallen from the seat as he sliced the restraint with the a dirk he always carried in his boot. He pulled her out of the window.

Her feet had been bare. She remembered with an awful clarity staring at her bare toes as Douglas shouted to her. Picking her up in his massive arms, he'd run towards the safety of the forest.

Why had he run?

Candace shook her head, willing the fog away.

He was a fool. But not a spy. She knew as well as she knew her own name that he'd never have betrayed Erik, never have betrayed her. But why, then, had he?

Her head rolled to the side on the cold stone. Small feet scurried across the floor. She didn't worry about the rats she was certain inhabited her prison. She was a country girl, born and bred. She knew there was far more to fear from two legged vermin than four.

She stared toward the spot where the door had closed, willing it to open, for the light to chase away the darkness. Even if only for a moment.

~~~

The feeling of Her leaving his mind like oil sliding thickly away always left him limp with relief. Wes let his shoulders relax under his tailored suit as he felt the distance between them widen, until he was free.

Or as free as he'd ever be.

He walked up the stairs to his quarters, passing silent servants and warriors alike. Fear was thick in the air. Marcus had been defeated. In the first battle of the war, they had lost. Badly.

He passed a sobbing woman, her pencil skirt pulled down over her knees as she huddled in a small corner of the rambling mansion. He paused next to her, recognizing her as a secretary, a pretty woman with a soft voice and heartsick eyes that followed one particular guard. "Do you require assistance?" He kept his voice low, respectful. She stiffened and wiped the tears from her cheeks.

"No, sir. I'm okay. Really." She gave him a patently false smile before standing and straightening her skirt. He watched her walk away, her fear of him greater than her need for comfort.

He continued up the stairs, his steps muffled by the thick rugs covering polished wood. The sun had long since set, but a full moon turned the walls silver. He paused before the door to his apartment dreading the silence waiting for him.

Always the silence.

He opened the unlocked door and crossed the threshold into the only sanctuary he possessed. He flicked on a light and walked through the empty room, removing his tie as he went.

Refurbishing the rooms had been a silent act of rebellion, a stubborn stance of individuality. Opening the door to his bedroom, he placed his tie on the waiting rack, removing his jacket before sitting on the ottoman at the foot of his bed and removing his shoes.

Setting them next to the bench, he made a mental note to leave them outside his door for polishing. He rested his forearms on his thighs and lowered his head. The peace that usually enveloped him when he entered his space evaded him. He pressed his palms to his eyes to erase the memory of ice blue eyes.

He lifted his head, his vision clearing, his hands itching. He stood and removed his shirt, folding it before placing it in the basket next to the closet. He unzipped his pants, emptying the pockets into the dish on his dresser. He lay them in the basket and then opened a drawer, digging around until he found what he was looking for.

He pulled out the faded red shirt, the lettering more space than text. He pulled it over his head and shuffled aside freshly pressed pajama pants until he was able to snag fleece pants that had seen better days. Donning the casual clothes felt like sliding into his own skin. He walked barefoot out of the bedroom and unlocked the door that led to his studio.

Once it had held a twin bed, a bookshelf, and a lonely desk. It had been emptied, the dark curtains replaced by sheer white drapes. The wooden floor was covered by a thick sail cloth. The only furnishing in the room stood in the center - a tall easel flanked by counter height oak tables stained in a kaleidoscope of paints.

He snagged a blank canvas from the pile against the wall and placed it on the easel. He stared at it as he readied his brushes, already seeing the image that had haunted him all day. He opened his paints and let the smell of oils cleanse him. He picked up a small remote and pressed a button sending music pounding through the room. Guitars wailed as he absently squeezed pigment onto a palette.

He emptied his mind, letting the music and paint lead his brush. Wide black strokes across snowy canvas built an outline. He was never sure what would flow from his brush, always surprised by the images it revealed. As drums pounded, the brush moved faster, almost frantically spreading gold and blue. Rose bloomed before his eyes while the drum beat quickened to match pace with his heartbeat.

His breath became ragged as the form revealed itself. Long, sleek lines framed a face concealed by a sweep of hair. He stepped back, chest heaving and eyes clearing to stare into blue eyes filled with fire.

He sat on the floor and stared up at her, recognizing desire thick as honey warming his stomach.

He dropped his brush to the floor, adding cool blue to the stained cloth.

"I am so screwed."

ABOUT THE PUBLISHER

Bannerwing Books is a collective of writing and editing professionals, founded in central Massachusetts in 2012. This independent publishing imprint now resides between three states across the USA.

Please visit us online at
www.bannerwingbooks.com

Made in the USA
Columbia, SC
19 December 2017